DREAM LAVENDER

A Lesbian Mystery Romance

Abby Frankenstein

Dedication

My first novel is dedicated to "Mother Rose." Patient, kind, and warm, Thanks.

About the Author

Abby Frankenstein is a fresh author, bringing her experience as a wandering woman into the imaginary world of fiction. "It is all true and all fiction," as Ernest Hemingway once said. Remaining curious, she has been surprised by life's turns and twists, swinging wildly from the thrilling and sublime to the dreary or microbe. Her first novel explores the possibilities.

Table of Contents

WRECKAGE!

Vivian was in control. She worked best on top. Her hands roved over Oceanna, driving her, raising her temperature, crushing her into a pile of desperate body parts that craved her. Viv's satin freckled breasts dragged over her neck, making Oceanna drool, thirsting for a deep drink from her lover's cup, her folds fragrant and hot. Large nipples tugged and sucked, pulled gently by teeth, thrilled them both.

Viv pulled herself up to straddle Oceanna's face. Smooth, fragrant thighs surrounded her lover's face. Plopping her puff of soft hair into her open mouth, she spread herself wide and wet. Twisting her hips, rolling over her face. She demanded Oceanna whip her to the finish.

Oceanna's own parts steamed as she parted Viv's folds with her tongue. Plunging her tongue deeply into Viv, tasting her water as it ran down her cheeks. Covered with her velvet, hearing her whispers, and feeling her desperation, her heart, and spirit entered the sublime. She dreamed of remaining forever in this madness.

Heavy breathing beckoned a soft word of direction, an urgent rustling. First slow, now fitful, and deep. Viv's chest filled, and she fell into a series of seizures. Her breaths gasped, then torrents whined and wailed. Her lungs blew out a siren, a scream, a blast!

Oceanna was pinned and began to panic. She felt a blunt blow and opened her eyes just in time to see the glint of chrome as the bright steel blade separated Viv's climaxing face from the rest of her. She strained to sit up and breathe. Viv's limp torso weighed heavily on her jaw, her dead muff squashing her howl. The decapitated torso collapsed, shifting the sensual bones across Oceanna's windpipe.

Blood, freed from all arterial confinement, gushed out of Viv's open neck, racing in the direction of gravity, spilling over the thighs and filling Oceanna's flaring nostrils. Her eyes rolled back in their sockets as she began to drown in her lover's blood. She thrust with all her might against what seemed like tons of flesh, violently twisting the body's shoulders, arms flailing like landed fish. She tugged and struck the still sweating corps with her bloody fists. She tossed one leg free of the blankets and over the edge of the bed, casting both bodies crashing to the floor.

Kicking her legs, she got free of the soaked sheets, knocking her skull on the worn wooden floor. Cussing, moaning, and crying, she yanked up her legs out from under poor Viv's knotted shoulder girdle that rolled and sagged as she displaced it. Slipping in the gore, she dragged herself to her knees through pools of warm blood. Retching and whimpering, she lifted her head to get a look at the murderer standing in the shadows, and there he was!

Tall and dark, he loomed at the foot of the bed, his flashing eyes sunk into a heavy brow, angular cheeks painted green and white fangs dripping blood were drawn in brightly, down to his rugged chin. Rocking back and forth like a ghoulish metronome, right, left, right, left, remaining mute.

Oceanna awoke, screaming, as she hit the hard cold floor. Sheets and blankets tossed during her nightmare tied her feet, strangling her circulation. Mouth open in a scream, she woke into a thick daze. She tried to get her bearings tangled, naked, sweating, and wheezing. Her lungs were straining to get a breath. She groped the side table, searching for her asthma inhaler. Confused, fizzy, and ready to faint, she fumbled over the side table, among wine glasses, ashtrays full of butts, tissues wet with tears, and gold-framed photos of Viv.

Gaudy photos that had been initially gifted to her old girlfriend, who later threw her out, smiled back at Oceanna in an assortment of lacey framed, eight by ten inch, black and white modeling portfolio photos. Instead of wasting them, Viv had impressed Oceanna with the theatrical "evening make-up," big hair, ruby lips, and dark shadow on eyelids expressing deep longing, shoulders exposed. Her lovesick eyes bounced briefly from one to the other. She grabbed her inhaler and sucked the medicine into her lungs.

"Nightmare. The same nightmare," she panted, took a moment, and relaxed. She admitted to herself that being mildly clairvoyant was inconvenient and could be dangerous.

Squinting through the dark, she caught the lit face of the rooster clock little Maria had found on a recent dumpster dive, proudly presenting the alarm clock with a peaceful image of a sunny farmyard on its face. Happy cows and horses munched and a rooster on a fence with yellow wings for dial hands, pointed to the numbers made up of vegetables, now reading 2:30 AM. Bar closing time. A pang of shame ran through her. She wondered where Vivian was sleeping tonight and again lambasted herself for worrying that the whore would dare to come back and hated that she would, of course, let her in.

Then she heard it, the floor squeaking at an even rhythmic pace. She was not alone. Flattening her belly on the floor, rolling under her bed, she grabbed the butt of her thirty-eight Snub-Nose hanging in a holster from the bed frame, pulled it out hard, and aimed at the silhouette of the man at the window.

Square-shouldered, rolling his body in a perfect rhythm, leaning to and froe, right, left, right left, Bob Smack focused on his mission. He remembered the last time he tried to help when he got in lots of trouble! This time he would get it right! This time he would get help! He faced her with his back to a large window and pointed.

"Bob! Damn, Bob Smack, what the hell are you doing? Scared me! I almost . . ."

She pulled herself up as the source of the yellow lights behind him pierced her eyes.

"Fire! Crap! Fire Bob! Call 911!"

"Fire!" Bob, echoing, now in a panic, heart pounding in his chest, rushed over, grabbed her arm with thick dry hands, and yanked her up to standing in one swift move.

"Call 911 now, like we practiced!" Grabbing her robe, she raced down the narrow stairs taking two at a time, fumbled the heavy front door latch with trembling hands, hauled open the door, pounded bare feet on the unpainted porch planks, and was stabbed by a thick splinter. Cussing the beastly old house for not fixing itself, bleeding as she limped, she crossed the street in the direction of Maria's house, ablaze.

C H A P T E R 2 :

FIRE!

Bob was transfixed for a moment by his own reflections in the series of Vivian's tall dressing mirrors standing around the room. Reflections of the flames flashed like diamonds, dancing over the walls. His own reflection was bedazzled by the shimmering lights and shadows. Jewels of light fluttered over his blocky shape, topped with his flat head, square jaw, and a heavy overhang of a brow. His face was still painted a ghastly cadaver green, fangs drawn by Maria, in bright white grease glowed on his patchily shaved chin. A convincing sinister image reflected off several walls, in his mind, casting him as an army.

Smelling the smoke and hearing the windy roar of air flashing into flame, he recalled the blistering heat as wood, cloth, and flesh turned to ash the last time he watched them burn. Old memories rolled around his head like a marble circling in a wide bowl. He side-stepped to the phone sitting on the table, picked up the receiver, and held it to his hairy ear.

The smoothness of the receiver felt silky in his chapped palm. He listened for the dial tone and tapped the buttons deliberately.

"9-1-1-." He envisioned the shapes of the numbers and followed the sequence perfectly this time. The tones tickled his eardrum, so he memorized each tone for later enjoyment.

"Emergency operator, what is your emergency, medical? Police or fire?" A professional female voice asked.

He braced himself, standing straight to emulate confidence.

"Help me! Bob Smack. Help!" Standing still, he could almost feel the flames and their duplicated reflections spinning over him, rolling up the walls and ceiling like being inside a giant kaleidoscope.

"What is the emergency, sir? Medical? Police or fire?"

"FIRE! Ahhh! FIRE!" He remembered now how to call.

Just then, he heard a faint voice, his name being yelled from the street below, and the wail of a distant siren drawing near. He dropped the receiver, raced down the hall, leaped down the narrow stairs, and streamed gracefully out the door, down the stone steps, and along the pavement to his mother. His beautiful mother, a long cigarette sticking from her lips, standing calmly in her nightgown, his overcoat draped across her shoulders, sucking, watching him gallop across the street to their rickety porch, like a statue.

Cruel glass shards jabbed into Oceanna's knees after she kicked the front door in, shattering the glass as she pounded her way into the front room of Maria's house. Black smoke billowed out of the door, collecting along the ceiling. Grime ground into her hands and knees as she crawled under the smoke toward Maria's bedroom in the rear of the home. She coughed hard, and her eyes burned.

Crayon drawings Maria crafted for her own 9th birthday were still taped on top of the mantle and fluttered in the hot wind. Pictures of her father riding a bucking bronc, chaps flapping, waving his wide-brimmed hat, with a comic-style balloon saying, "Happy Birthday Maria." Ralfie had been on the road, Maria had made a card for him to give her, knowing he had wanted to be with her.

Burning ceiling tiles fell in front of Oceanna as she crawled through the living room. She shut her eyes as they fell almost on top of her. Ducking under the coffee table, she scattered half a dozen beer cans and several sample perfume bottles that clattered over the floor in her panic. Peeking out, she recognized the large handbag on the floor in front of her with Vivian's name tag hanging from the shoulder strap. A small plaque declaring "Top CozmetixX sales." Viv's "Toys for Joys" logo strung about the abused handle. Her expensive high heel shoes tumbled among fancy ostrich-skin cowboy boots under the couch. Worn out socks and silver stockings, shed in a hurry, topped the pitiful pile.

"Son of a bitch!" she mumbled as she belly-slithered under the coffee table to the bedroom doors. The black smoke was building above her. She made it to Ralfie's bedroom door and tried the doorknob, but it was too hot. She pushed, but it would not budge. She called out with no answer, rolled onto her back, and kicked the door, hitting the soft wood with her bare feet. Kicking over and over, burning her feet, scorching her lungs, with a breaking heart. She wondered as she drifted into blackness, how in the hell the worst had worsened.

C H A P T E R   3 :

SURPRISE!

S ix months earlier:

Maria shook the cassette tape vigorously to free it of the dumpster dust it had collected at the bottom of the trash. She rattled the loops of tape.

"I don't think I can save this one, Bob," she squinted at the reels through the murky plastic case. "It's smashed."

Bob pulled out a thin rolling paper, sprinkled a pinch of tobacco along it with yellow fingers, rolled them into a lumpy cylinder, and licked the glue for a seal. Rolling it between his fingers, he held it to his hairy ear listening to the grind of the leaves. Packed too tight and a poor draw. He stuck the cigarette between his thin lips and waited for a light from his partner, not being trusted with a lighter of his own. Waggling it up and down, he hoped to get her attention, but she was too busy goofing with the entertainment.

"Hey, macho loco, make me one too! You roll, um, better than I do," she leaned over the warped plywood they had scrounged for their clubhouse table. "You look so big and mean, but you are nice, and I am so small but really so terrible! Look how big your hands are. Hold it up, come on." She lifted his hand from the rolling papers and spread his fingers out like a fan. She matched her delicate palm to his thick, calloused one.

"Your fingers are twice as thick. I'm skinny but strong. Look, feel my arm," she flipped her messy black braids over her shoulder and rollup up her tee-shirt sleeve, bent her arm, and flexed her wiry arm to bring up her bicep.

"Feel that!" She grinned at him with determination.

He gripped her arm with his hot hand, enfolding it like a blanket, using his finger to tickle her armpit. She laughed and pulled away.

Bob began to rock his body right and left while vibrating his smoke out of frustration. The rivets in his bent lawn chair creaked under his weight.

Maria dug deep into the front pocket of her worn jeans, pulled out her prized metal lighter, flicked open the silver lid with a ring, drew the flint wheel along her blue jeans fast, creating a dazzling spark, bursting the wick into flame, lit the end of his smoke, blew out the flame, flicked the lid shut with a bang and back in her pocket with panache. The odor of fuel filled the room. Maria overfilled it on a daily basis, whether it needed it or not.

"You are tough, but I am agile. That's why we are a good team, right?" She smiled at him.

Bob blinked his eyes rapidly at her in agreement. He inhaled the smoke deeply, handed it to Maria, and began rolling another two or three cigarettes for later.

"I think we are addicted," she said.

He didn't respond with a blink or a nod.

"Ok. Play cards, right? I will tell your fortune."

Nimble fingers shuffled the worn Tarot deck using fancy alternating mixing styles. Flashing a card, now and then, spreading the deck in a pattern in front of Bob on the rough wood surface.

"Pick a card, sir," she grinned for a second, then froze in mid-dealing.

Suddenly, Bob sprung up like a life-sized Jack-in-the-Box to his full height, slamming his skull into the floor joists above him in the low basement, just missing a drainpipe. Maria ducked at the sound of thick wood meeting thick bone. Tears came to Maria's eyes, thinking he may be cracked. Bob just stood, stunned.

"Crap, are you alright?" She whimpered, smashing out the butt with her boot.

Bob's dark eyes stared at the smudged basement window, level with the driveway surface, looking for movement. His ears focused on the sound of a car coming up the driveway. Tires creeping along the broken cement, grinding along at a stealthy pace. A puffing engine, puttering with an exhaust leak, rolling slowly, closer.

"Cops! Hide!" she whispered.

CHAPTER 4:

RATS, RACOONS, AND BATS, OH MY!

Pulling her '67 Dodge Dart into the driveway, Oceanna eyed the steep roof needing shingles topping the three-story Queen Anne architecture. She followed the tall river stone chimney flanking the spectacular stained glass octagonal turret with fluttering bats hiding among its beams. The peeling paint was not too bad, and the pillars standing around the wide stone porch were straight. The garden was dark with overgrown blackberry vines, lined with thorns as long as a cat's claws, and she mumbled to herself, "Yikes."

She continued up over the cracked cement to a level spot in front of the tumble-down garage. Tangles of blackberry vines wove in and around the laurel hedge along the boundaries between Grandma's place and the house next door, clogging the driveway and scratching her doors. The vines wound around her tires, tugging the vines, driving clouds of brown house sparrows from their nests. They rocketed out, flapping and peeping, startling Oceanna.

"Perfect. Wildlife too. As long as there are no rats or raccoons," the engine sputtered as she cut it off. Reattached the heater hose at her feet that fell off on long trips. Vines stabbed into her calves through her jeans as she struggled to avoid them. Red stripes of blood oozed from scratches through her socks as she struggled to walk over the vines that bounced and clung with each step.

"Note to self, cut the vines," she mumbled.

Pulling the ring of three skeleton keys from her pocket, she examined them. They were tarnished black and as long as her palm.

"Well, let's see what they fit. I don't remember all this. It has been forever," she said to herself.

She circled down the driveway to the front porch steps, steep and made of large stones. Long climbing rose bushes overgrew the flower beds. Tendrils lay across the steps with big red roses weighing them down, creating a carpet of bright petals, bees buzzing throughout. It looked beautiful and dangerous. She shuddered. A tingle went up her spine. The keys felt hot in her hand.

Tip-toeing around the roses and bees, she carefully climbed the stairs to the wooden porch. The wide planks were solid but rough. Lilac hedges grew thick over the rails. Sweet violet blossoms giving perfume to the shadows they cast, alive with the buzzing, black and yellow harvesters of pollen bobbing in and out.

She remembered the wide door, especially the cast iron door latch in the shape of a lion's face, its tongue sticking out to be thumbed after the key was turned. It was at her eye level when she was five years old, she was given the job of pulling the lion's tongue down to help Grandmother Blanch.

Images of Blanche popped up in her mind. Short flashes of events that seemed happy now recalled as lonely. She recalled looking through the window of the oven while the cookies baked, chasing cats running from her as she pounded the floor in her socks. Flashbacks of gauzy curtains, lazily fluttering in the large windows in summer, sun flooding in, making bright hot puddles on the floor just the right size for napping.

She fumbled with the ring of keys to sort out the right one. One of the long skeletons slid in easily and turned with a clank. She thumbed the lion's tongue and shoved the heavy door open. The smell of Grandma's incense filled her nostrils.

CHAPTER 5:

THE TOWER!

"Hello?" she called instinctively, pushing the door open with a squeak. Sage incense, roses, and patchouli oil permeated the air. The oily fragrances had soaked into the wood floors, bringing out the smell of pine and polish even a year after Blanche's death. The room was clean but cluttered, with photos in frames on the walls and set around side tables and the fireplace mantle. Oceanna remembered they had always been there looking back at her. Blanche had many followers.

She wanted to touch everything, and when she did, images came to her. Flashing for a second with no obvious connection to each other. Just faces and ghosts.

"Gone but not forgotten," she whispered back at them. Hearing the mantra flow into her head, she felt compelled to recite it again, without connection, just fragments, hints. She breathed in deeply. Intentionally letting the smells trigger images, associations, and reactions. She smacked her lips to taste them. The atmosphere was charged. She felt detached, as though she had slipped out of the solid world into the magical realm and was carried off.

"No, no. Keep hold. Stay on the ground," she warned the mysterious part of herself that sometimes pulled her out of the solid into the mystical. The invitation to wander into mystery scared and fascinated her. She focused hard to remain connected to the solids, kicking off her shoes to run her toes along the carpet, to feel the hardness of the floor under her.

She ran her hands over the furniture, traced the window frames with her fingers, and touched the grain in the wood of a large dining room table, flower vases, and her dusty old favorite Player Piano.

Opening the lid of the faded bench, she found scrolls ready to be played, carefully concealed in their original boxes, song titles on their labels. Her favorite is still on top. Blue Velvet. She carefully lifted it out, shut the lid, and opened the box to greet the yellow perforated paper scroll that had filled the house with music, pushing her into the past vividly.

Recalling the feeling of childhood, the slippery bench under her butt, stretching her toes to reach the peddles, pushing to help her grandmother move the bellows that rolled the scroll and pounded the keys. She could feel her grandmother's shoulder next to her and saw the black and white keys popping up and down as if by an invisible hand. She felt the ring of the notes in her ears. She remembered singing in a high voice, trying to match the song, then laughing and begging grandmother to play it again. Blanche's face smiling back, laugh lines deepening as she gave in, winding the scroll back onto its dowel, then pumping the peddles and playing it all again. She was beautiful and emanated a strange, convincing allure.

Oceanna laughed out loud, jolting herself from the mist.

"What?" she called out, transitioning back from the past. Was that her name being called? She looked around, expecting to see someone behind her. Sitting still on the bench, she focused, listening for a clue. The house was still. No sounds of traffic in the street or dogs barking at the mailman, or yelling of children at play. She shook her head, rubbed her brow, and stood.

"Stay on the ground. Just memories, nothing to hurt. Nothing weird, all is well," she mumbled.

The door to a narrow staircase caught her eye. The tight spiral stairs leading to the turret beckoned. A chill ran up her back.

She slowly climbed the tight stairs that spiraled up steeply in short triangular steps along a curved wall. Inhaling deeply, she slid the slender pocket door open, revealing a bright cylindrical room with floor-to-ceiling windows lining the tower, and shelves filled with books.

Volumes on medicine, women, witchcraft, astronomy, nature, and the supernatural crammed the walls. Heavy leather-bound books with hand-painted plates of birds and bugs and landscapes piled along the edges of the shelves, being too big to set in. Books about religions, wisdom, poems and spells, the Tarot, and meditation were stuffed in, squeezed into the tower's intricate frame. The 180-degree overlook offered views of the southeast neighborhood. The wide view looked down at the yards and houses, following west, down Belmont Street, over the Willamette River to the sparkling Portland city towers, ending at the West Hills.

The high ceiling was fashioned of wood beams in an intricate design. A spindly mobile dangled thorny rose stems tied with black thread counter balanced with maple leaves dried and curled, tipping in the slightest breeze, crackling as they bumped into each other. She took a deep breath and blew at it from across the room, creating just enough disturbance to cause the leaves to bob.

Tall candles sat on the antique table in the center of the room. The oval tabletop was decorated with a beautiful hand-painted astrological calendar and a simple wooden box with a deck of worn Tarot cards covered with a piece of red velvet sitting inside and a set of wooden chairs.

Oceanna remembered the room, the atmosphere, the windows, and the long black velvet couch along one wall she had played on. Smells of ritual herbs that had been burned still lingered, sandalwood and lavender.

Fragrant smoke left oils that were absorbed by the leather books and wooden beams, giving the room a polished, waxy sheen to the surfaces. The aged luster suggesting a passionate life, romantic, artistic, and deep in spirit. Oceanna could feel and taste it.

Her naked toes cured along the worn surface of the wide wooden planks of the floor as she was emersed in images of Blanche sitting in the chair at the table, absorbed in thought while setting the cards in a particular order on the table, her long gray hair tumbling over her shoulders, her cheeks lined but blushing as she found the answers among her cards and books.

Then echoing whispers filtered into the room. Oceanna stopped to listen, trying to discern if they were real. Shuffling sounds and what could have been footfall vibrated into the floor. She moved to the iron heater vent capping the conduit leading from the basement. There seemed to be motion below. Her heart began to pound, and the room's beauty faded from her thoughts.

Reaching into her jean pocket, she fumbled, found her inhaler, and puffed the medicine into her tightening bronchus. It stung but gave relief. Something was afoot. She slid the pocket door closed and descended the spiral stairs, along the kitchen floor, then into the basement stairs silently. The balls of her feet acting as pillows, quietly plopping along the wood, sneaking.

Rivulets of perspiration ran down Maria's ribs. The perspiration dampened her face, collecting dust from the dirty couch she hid under, making a muddy mask over her face. Nose hairs resembled bee's knees loaded with pollen and itching. Clear ooze ran down from her nostrils to her upper lip. The crown of her scalp held up the stinky cushion, an inch or so, giving her a gap between the frame of the couch and the seat to see through as someone came closer, descending the basement stairs. Her eyes watered, blurring her vision. She shook with anticipation.

CHAPTER 6:

THE CLUB HOUSE

Bob heard the footsteps descending, getting closer. Quiet feet. Soft. He listened closely to the emotion in the approach. Light and careful. Not like his Dad. Not angry. Small.

Hiding in the metal cabinet reminded him of his childhood, hiding cross-legged in the rear of his mother's closet, listening to his father's ugly temper. He often created his own comfortable world among her meticulously arranged shoes, not in matching pairs but by his own unique aesthetics. Friendly Barbie dolls, well dressed, sat in them, laces tied, pink plastic toes pointed, arms raised in stiff "Hellos," chatting amongst themselves. They respectfully avoided commenting about the punishment. He rocked side to side, letting the movement sweep him along, soothing thoughts, mentally distancing him to a safe location, immunization to vulnerability.

Now, bracing his back against the metal locker, peering through the vent in the door, Bob felt the tears trickle down his cheek. It had been long since he felt hunted, isolated, and holding still, but his nerves began to break. He felt the rage. Panic set in. He wet himself when he felt the basement stairs jiggling with the stranger's descent.

Oceanna panted with anxiety. Holding a frying pan for protection in front of her, creeping down the dry staircase, squinting in the dimness, hoping she was safe.

"What are the odds that some creep is hiding in the basement?" she thought. "Nothing is disturbed, nothing taken. Nobody is going to just live in a basement and not take stuff."

Reaching the last stair, she paused to listen and look. Rolling papers and tobacco were scattered over a makeshift table, and a candle was stuck in a bottle. Soda cans were stacked in several pyramids along the dirt floor and the stone foundation. A set of checkers and a deck of tarot cards were spread around the table and floor. An ashtray was tipped over with a but still smoldering, indicating a very recent visitor. She began to wheeze. She looked over her shivering shoulder. The metal cabinet in the corner shuddered and squeaked. Startled, she dropped the frying pan with a clatter.

A high-pitched voice calling franticly from the street.

"Bob-eee! Come home, Bob-eee!"

What was left of Bob's nerves shattered. He slammed open the metal door violently and rocketed out from the box, crying, wet, and screaming for his mother. He rammed Oceanna aside, sweeping his arms wildly. He charged out the secret basement door onto the driveway and into the street, wailing.

Oceanna, stunned by the speed of a wild man, mouth wide open, eyes gleaming, tossed her like a rag doll over the lawn chairs and onto the plywood table, bowling over the milk crate supports. The wood dropped over her. While she passed out, she lay crumpled, wheezing, and fading to black. She thought she heard cussing in Spanish and smelled the sour odor of urine.

Maria dared to lift the cushion covering her head and found herself face-to-face with a blacked-out Oceanna.

"Holey crap!" she said while considering that she now had a chance to really give first aid.

C H A P T E R   7 :

NEIGHBORLY INTRODUCTION

After dragging Oceanna out of the basement and onto the un-mowed crabgrass, Maria tried to remember the list of do's and don'ts on the Cardiopulmonary Resuscitation poster when the girl scout troop was learning First Aide. Misty memories of the pictorial instructions came to mind now that she strained to recall them. She regretted making fun of the recuse-dummy's rubbery mouth, sticking her fingers up its translucent rubber nostrils, and pretending to pick it. Entertaining the girls was a thrill for Maria and more than an annoyance to the scout mothers. She had been uninvited to come back. Maria decided to course correct, leaving her budding comedy career for one in medicine.

Oceanna's head began to clear. She felt the scratches and bruises from being dragged out along the rough pavement. Her wrists felt sore as Maria pressed too firmly while seeking a pulse, cutting off the throb and leaving her with the impression that Oceanna had no pulse and was dead.

Leaning over Oceanna's face, her ear almost touching lips, she tried to feel breath on her cheek and see if the chest was rising and falling.

"Stop, or I'll shoot!" came a harsh voice from behind. "Son of a bitch, what the hell is going on!"

The hair on her neck stood on end. Maria flung her body back away from Oceanna, landing on her knees across the grass. Through her tangled bangs, she saw slender knees covered in black fishnet stockings bordered by the high hem of a black leather mini skirt. White fingers with long black nails gripped a can of mace aimed at her face.

"Help! Call 911! Fire! Rape!" Vivian yelled. Her hands were shaking, and her high heels dug into the grass, causing her to stumble.

"She is alive! Help!" Maria covered her face with her arm and kicked at the mace can held down at her level. The toe of her cowboy boot collided with the hand, spinning Vivian like a top and shooting a stream of mace into Oceanna's face creating a howl of pain.

Her eyes were on fire, blind and disoriented. She cavorted and rolled into the overgrown flower garden. Maria crawled to the tangled garden hose on a rusty reel and turned the water on as the pinched hose dripped. Vivian pulled out her heels, chased Maria, and grabbed her from behind as the police drove up.

The bulbous end of her dirty nose bumped along the shiny gold badge, leaving a greasy smear across its perfect finish. The officer poured cold water across her face, into her red-hot eyes and burning throat, and pulled Vivian and Maria apart. After settling Vivian in the back seat of the cruiser for safety and assigning Maria to the porch, she asked what had happened. Each participant shared the details, dried tears, and laughed about the mess.

When the stories had been exhausted, they shook hands and introduced themselves, Oceanna and Vivian, as the new ladies of the haunted house. Maria and her father, Ralfie, referred to themselves as a "rodeo family" and discussed the rules of friendship. Maria toyed with the idea of getting them to watch her when her father was at the rodeo.

The emergency team snapped their kits shut with a series of clicks and rolled down the street silently. Maria and her father waved goodbye and retreated to their house, leaving Oceanna and Vivian standing in the driveway. The flock of house sparrows was still among the berry bushes, and the street was vacant of looky-loos.

"Well, we have introduced ourselves to the neighbors, I guess," said Oceanna, wiping her mouth with a wet cloth. Her eyes were still blurry from the spray. Her shirt was caked with grass, and her elbows were red from the fray.

"Right. Very fancy," said Viv as she yanked her high heels out of the sod. "They are ruined."

She pushed her long black hair over her torn blouse sleeve and held the mud-smeared pumps up for inspection.

"Welcome home, darling," spreading her arms and pointing to the old structure looming before them. She slipped her arm around Viv's narrow waist and pulled her close. "And it's haunted."

"All this and more?" she smiled. "I need a drink," she kissed Oceanna on her reddening cheek.

"You maced me."

"You deserved it."

"I need a shower and a drink," Oceanna looked down at her stained front and laughed.

"Great! Let me help you," Viv kissed her on the lips.

Standing behind the tangled bushes, Bob watched, rocking to his soothing rhythm. Right, left, right, left. Dry berries and leaves crunching under his cob nail boots. He watched the women cuddle close together.

CHAPTER 8:

AMBROSIA

"Right, left. Right, left. Right, left." Bob hummed his soothing song. Acorns and the blackened remains of berry seeds ground into dust under his weight. Standing behind the thick veil of vines, amongst the piles of rotting leaves and overgrown weeds, enjoying the brittle symphony, Bob watched the warmth they shared. With the skill developed over a lifetime of hiding and watching, he could remain safe and secure at a distance.

He was just a boy when he was committed to the mental hospital with the proud announcement on the sign on the front gate, "Asylum for feeble-minded." Growing up inside was going to prove spectacular. He remembered the tall, blank brick walls, dark windows with bars, and cement floors left bare for easy cleaning. Water hoses turned on people who soiled themselves cried too much, demanded attention, or fought back.

The staff, dressed in sterile white, patrolling through the wards, jingling keys to doors that rang metallic as they shut behind. Bob was haunted by voices echoing off the green cinderblock walls. He learned to appreciate the soulful accompaniment from the reverberation of voices, calling, crying, and wanting. He understood he was fortunate and helped those who could not walk or see.

At times of wanting warmth, his favorite nurse's face came to mind. Her frizzy blond hair was pulled in a tight bun, drawn back under her nursing crown. Strands of hair came undone as the shift went on. Silky straggles coming loose from donning and doffing her stethoscope from her large ears, giving her a frazzled look by the end of the day. Her broad yellowing smile enchanted him with her coral lipstick. The color generously smeared, light blue eye shadow to contrast her bloodshot eyes, and red rouge on the sagging apples of her cheeks, entrancing him.

Bob's eyes fluttered nervously, recalling being punished for settling his gaze on her obvious cleavage. He noticed Nurse Ambrosia's name tag was crooked. She coyly confronted him, standing in scuffed white wedges, as tall as his chin, leaning so close to his belt he could feel her sagging breasts crammed into tight white lace. Edges of the folding money she kept there showed as a lure just above the graying elastic. Bob understood.

Tired Ambrosia smoked like a chimney, drank like a fish, cussed like a sailor, smelled cheap, was cruel to the patient, and had sex in their beds when she found a guard that was longing when no one was watching except Bob. He loved Nurse Ambrosia.

"I'm gonna do you a favor, Bobby. I'm gonna give you secrets of how to keep a woman happy. You're just a 10-year-old boy, but that is no excuse for bad manners," she gave a raspy laugh and looked right at him. "You're just the type that can make a woman happy, someday, if one will have ya. You've got talent, Bob! You are strong and stupid, and you never say noth'in. That is the most important part, Bob! Little known! Little known!"

She lectured him as she sat at the nursing desk, counting out the pills, dropping them into small white paper cups, and tossing one pill into her mouth as needed. Spinning the chair to face him, she spread her legs as wide as she could, enticing him to look up at her wrinkled uniform so she could scold him for being lewd. Discipline was the first phase of her training.

"After offending a woman, you must make amends. That's proper, right? You have got to learn boundaries!" She shook her finger at him. "After passing the pills, I'm gonna show ya." He rocked back and forth and fluttered his eyelids. "I was hoping you'd say that."

She took time to teach Bob the things he needed to know; how to rub her swollen ankles, how to massage her shoulders, how to clean the toilets and showers late at night, and how to make the beds so tight a quarter could bounce. She taught him how to make a passable Screwdriver cocktail from little bottles of vodka in her purse and stolen orange juice lifted off the breakfast trays.

Like all great teachers, she protected and rewarded her favorite pupil. He would not have to take the pills that numbed his mind and body. If he were good, he received fewer restraints than the rest, and he got to "watch out" for Nurse when she had a "date."

"Bob Smack? You even got a shity name. You got all the breaks," she said as she twiddled her bare feet resting on his bed pillow. She smirked at Bob as he wrung his hands and rocked from one flat foot to another, standing just inside the open closet door.

"You're even too ugly for your mother to love, baby," her bulging eyes slid lazily under thick lids in his direction. Grinning at him with thick lips parted over sticky teeth slowly like a breaking banana, she said, "You know who loves ya around here, though, right? You're a perfect boyfriend for me, Bob. You're mute as hell, and you smoke my brand."

Bob halted his rocking for a Moment.

"What would I do without you?" Downing the final dregs of the cough syrup prescribed to Bob, she added, "And I hold the keys." The outer door alert beeped, keys jingled, and footsteps came down the hall. "Oh, take your place. He's coming. And stop rocking. I can hear hangers."

Five shirts and five black pants divided the closet in half. He stood in the gap between them, and she closed the closet door and locked it. Bob concentrated on being still. He positioned one eye to look out one-half of the small vent in the door. Standing bravely and still, poised at attention, as ordered. He viewed her carnal activities secretly, like a knight through his visor. His shield a closet door. His kingdom is a locked ward. His beloved queen, Nurse Ambrosia. His mission is to watch.

CHAPTER 9:

ZIG-ZAG

Her hair shone like black cornsilk. Every strand of Vivian's bouncy cascade became organized into wavy rows with the pull and pass of the comb. The CozmetixX-enhanced shine of her hair reflected the headlights, shimmering like the raindrops and slick mountain road they sped down this night.

Oceanna's eyes wandered from the road now and then as she admired the preparation as much as the finished product. Her heart fluttered. She craved a smoke. The old Dodge glided.

Pulling down the visor to check her make-up in the mirror, Viv's hair floated along her cheeks, resting around the uncovered shoulders and down her back like a fine stole. Several perfect curls turned up around and down into the smooth freckled satin of her healthy cleavage.

Captivated like an addict getting a rush, she traced her lover's shape in short glances. Pupils wide, Oceanna found herself enslaved. She was compelled to answer any request.

"Thank you, babe." Viv purred. "So, you'll do it?"

"Do? What's to do? You already know her. We go to every gig possible, every dinky town, every dive in Portland and beyond. Look how far Zig-Zag is," she swerved a bit. The wipers clanked rhythmically across her dreamy eyes, smearing spring bugs into solution.

"I'm turning up the heater in here. My hair needs to dry."

Thumbing the Dart's antique chrome knobs and leavers, she dragged the heater lever from mostly defrost to mostly floor and flicked the dial from Lo to Hi.

"She hasn't purchased much, though. I need to do her stage face . . . and her hair . . . still a mullet, please. You know the whole band could use a little upgrade too, but Sunny is the star out front. She needs to look at it, I think. She is your friend; don't you want to help her be her best? A woman that talented and handsome should show it, right?"

"And . . . you have a crush on her, Viv. Let's not forget that."

"I am talking very seriously about business right now. God! I am busting my ass making this business work, and you're jealous and edgy and dragging your feet on supporting me!" She smacked Oceanna's knuckles with the sharp ends of the comb teeth.

"Hey! Now I have tooth marks on my knuckles to match the ones on my . . ."

Viv snatched her sleeve and shook her arm violently, spinning the steering wheel, causing the car to swerve over the white edge line and tearing a cufflink off Oceanna's dress shirt. The front wheels slid on the gravel berm. Mud and rocks ricocheted from the tire to the fender, blasting the metal.

Elbowing Viv away, she regained control of the car with several wide sweeps, steering back onto the pavement. The Momentum rolled their bodies back and forth over the slick leather upholstery, bouncing Viv off the metal doors until the friction of the breaks slowed them safely, onto a wide spot in a path of a Christmas tree farm, off the roadside, to a stop. The Dodge purred quietly. The wipers continued to bang. The women panted to catch their breaths.

"Damn it, Viv! You're gonna kill us before we get there," she glared at Viv, still straight-arming a brace against the dashboard. "You agreed no more hitting. I hate that."

Oceanna pulled out an asthma inhaler and puffed several shots into her lungs. Her heart began to settle. Then pulled out a couple of cigarettes from her pocket, lit them with the dashing lighter, and handed one to Viv. Vivian took the smoke without looking at her.

For a couple of minutes, they sat silently, just the low hum of the engine, the slap of the wipers, and the patter of the rain surrounding them in the tree-lined dark.

"I'm trying to establish a place for myself in business, Anna," Viv turned her body to face her. Her eyes flashed with intensity. "Look at me, Anna," she was firm but smooth. "I flirt as part of my approach. People like flattery. It is welcoming. I am trying to offer an enhanced experience. A change that makes a difference in their lives. The presentation is important in show business, especially for women, as you well know."

Oceanna looked into the eyes of her lover, feeling the pull, wanting to be convinced that loving her was safe. Wanting to believe, wanting to feel her kiss.

"You share more of yourself than you should," she said.

"When the money starts rolling in, you won't say that. But it means more to me than just sales. It is my own business, and it's Show Business. I'm ambitious. I am putting my all into it to ensure success. It's a way into something bigger! I want to be part of the show business world. I need you to support me and help me. We've had this talk. It's not a surprise."

Popping open the glove box, she pulled out tissues and patted the tears that started to run down her cheeks, careful not to pull off her powder or smear her mascara. She slammed the cover shut with a bang, startling Oceanna as she pouted.

"You are jealous and insecure. I got that!" She stamped out her smoke hard, almost bending the ashtray. "I have to be able to breathe! You have to trust me."

Oceanna started to cry. "You are gorgeous and wonderful, and you attract lots of admirers. That's the curse that comes with loving beauty. I know that" Viv handed her a tissue. "Okay, what exactly do you need me to do? Tell me again."

She pulled herself close and put her arm around her shoulders. The widows fogged up.

"I need to get them to listen to my pitch, especially Sunny's wife, Kelly. She's the manager. She is the one that promotes. You are close to her. I need to discuss the potential merits of CozmetixX on the band. Don't overdo it. I just need a chance, Anna. Just a chance."

The tears stopped flowing as she felt Viv's hips against her side. She felt the tingle of her breath close to her ear and the smell of her hair as it brushed her neck.

"We are going to be fine. We are going to this gig, and we are going to rub shoulders with "Sunny Moon and the Satellites," and we are going to drink and dance and have fun. Right?"

Oceanna nodded and felt the glow return. "Right," she whispered. "We are gonna schmooze," She turned her face to be nose to nose. "I'm in love with you, Viv."

"I know that, darling. So, support my dream," she kissed her on the corner of her mouth. "We might get to Hollywood," she whispered, giving her a long deep kiss. "Now, get this bucket of bolts racing. I hate to be late. And that'll piss me off," she laughed.

"Yes, Ma'am!" Sloppily wiping the windshield from the fog with her free palm, she yanked the car into drive and hit the gas.

Viv pulled her lover's hand up her thigh and under her skirt. "Don't take your eyes off the road, babe. We'll talk when we get home, okay?" All Oceanna could do was nod and smile.

They flew down the serpentine road, passing the carved wooden sign designating the entry into the tiny town of Zig-Zag and into the dirt parking lot of the rustic all-night honkytonk called The Sawmill.

Beloved and lifted 4X4 pickup trucks spattered with mud decorated the parking lot. Big tires with toothy treads scattered thick dirt over the hood and windshields, driven by hearty woodsmen to a bar and a dance. Flashy sports cars and glistening motorcycles lined in rows crowded the lot. The Dodge bounced among the potholes.

Vivian clutched her bag and asked to be let out at the front door to spare her new high heels and hair. Several bearded men smoking pot near the bouncer's stool chuckled and eyed her. She asked for a light and smoked among them confidently while Oceanna hunted for a parking spot. She joked with the barrel-chested money collector at the door. She admired his tattoos and discussed music, dropping Sunny's band member's names while batting her eyelashes, getting them in for free.

By the time Oceanna made her way through the downpour to the front door, the big man was calling them by name like an old friend. He hauled open the door and waved a hand signal to the lady bartender, who nodded back, getting their first round of drinks on his tab. He yelled over the jukebox music that Oceanna was a lucky woman as she passed.

She shook her head in amazement. Vivian was radiant when she was on.

C H A P T E R   1 0 :

THE SAWMILL

Under green and purple stage lights, the dim room vibrated with a crowd ready for the music to start. The neon beer signs glowed behind the bar. Illuminated and animated, the rolling blueness of cascading waters and trotting Clydesdale horses somehow suggest the beer's quality. Large neon beer signs hung high on the walls casting light on the high peak of the Sawmill's ceiling. The bathroom doors decorated intricately with deer leaping over logs, reading "Bucks" and "Does."

Giant rusty saw discs, used in the mill during its years of operation, were displayed and bolted to the original pine log construction. Double-headed axes and long falling saws with handles on each end for human engines to operate adorned each wall, looming like brown ghosts of the pioneer past.

Images of the old logger teams that had built the place were remembered in long black-and-white pictures preserved in carved frames. Proud and rugged workers determined to make it. Museum-quality photos of woodmen straddling huge trees and teams of mules pulling heavy loads hung all along the walls.

Burning briskly with a yellow glow was the real treasure of the bar, a monumental river rock fireplace twelve feet across with a yawning hearth that burned logs four feet long. A worthy German mason engineered the efficient masterpiece both to warm the entire mill and show off his artistry.

He included every color of local stone in a complex rustic mosaic. A photo of him, bearded, muscled, and gripping his tools, sat on the thick hand-hewn mantel.

Arranged on the low wooden stage were a bright gold saxophone, a highly polished red bass guitar, a worn black six-string guitar, and microphones on stands. A silver drum set was being assembled by a long-haired drummer, tightening the screws and tuning tom-tom heads. He lifted his gaze and spun a drumstick "hello" at Vivian while they stood at the bar collecting a tray full of drinks for the band.

Oceanna lifted the tray with six White Russians, two for Viv, two apricot brandies for herself, and twelve Slippery Nipples to offer the ladies that ended up sharing their table. Viv tipped the hard woman mixing the drinks with a smile, a wink, and a twenty-dollar bill.

As they wove across the crowded room, around chairs and tables filled with partiers, to a high table against the wall, they passed the drummer. Viv lifted a couple of drinks from the tray and handed one to him with panache, wished him broken legs, and lingered at the edge of the stage. Continuing across the wide polished plank dance floor, Oceanna caught her reflection in the mirrors on the stage's backdrop. Her short hair was sticking up, wet and windblown, but her pants were fitting well, so she didn't worry. With a shapely backside, mussy hair was forgiven.

She reached the high round table with a collection of stools with a paper sign reading, "Reserved for the band." She slid several brands of cigarettes already dropped into a pile to one side, set down the tray, and squinted into the audience hunting for familiars. The waterfall beer clock behind her read 9 o'clock.

"Perfect timing," she mumbled to herself, glugged down one of the Slipper Nipples, and chewed the cherry.

Two sneaky, confident hands slid themselves on either side of her hips from behind. Long fingers slipped into her suspender buttons, hooking on. Small breasts pressed against her wet back, and a low velvet voice whispered close into her chilled red ears.

"Let's never quit meeting like this, my drowned cat. Guess who."

"Humm . . . are you smart?" she played.

"A very smart ass," the voice purred.

"Are you ravishing?"

"So, you have told me."

"Are you a big pain in my . . .?" Oceanna downed another drink and held the cherry between her teeth.

"Shut up and hand me a drink, you turd!" said her captor. A delicate hand adorned with an extravagant ruby ring slipped past her elbow and clutched a brandy.

"I propose a toast. I'm a proud haunted house owner," slowly twisting her body around so as not to spill the table, she rotated to face her embracer. A pale face smirked back at her, brought her lips up to the stem of the cherry sticking out of Oceanna's smile, took the stem into her teeth, pulled the fruit out of her mouth slowly, and ate it.

"I told you Viv was a witch. Now you have a house to put her in," Kelly grinned and chewed.

"I'm telling Sunny you're jealous," she said. "How was that fancy honeymoon anyway, Kel?"

Kelly's attention was drawn to the activity on the stage. Her cocoa-brown eyes jerked away from tracing Oceanna's disheveled hair to focus tightly on a point over Oceanna's shoulder. The colored stage lights were being tested.

"Hang on, Anna, a manager's work is never done. I want a hot red light on her," she smiled at Oceanna. "Order us another bunch of drinks, and I'll be back to catch up," Kelly untangled herself from the closeness. "You gonna make the whole show?" she asked softly. Anna nodded a self-conscience yes.

Turning professional, Kelly edged through the impatient audience, putting her hand on their shoulders, thanking them for coming as she went. Finally, she flagged the drummer, enlisting him as a grip, disconnecting Vivian abruptly from him.

Oceanna could see her annoyed smile as she greeted Kelly diplomatically. The pantomime continued. Viv needed her to feel positive about her. She bowed and apologized for distracting him, bobbing her head and touching Kelly's sleeve. Oceanna could see she was nervous even from this distance in the dark.

"Well, Viv is mixing with a master. She ought to learn something," she mumbled. And waved her hand to flag the waitress for another tray of drinks.

Vivian stood behind Kelly and tried to position herself among the activities. Kelly hugged her tight to reassure her for Oceanna's sake and directed her back to the table.

"My God. She got the squeeze! She may pull this off yet," feeling the alcohol relaxing her nerves, she wondered if she should fasten her seat belt, bracing for a bumpy ride, or just let the chips fall where they may and leap.

The performance was delicious, as usual. Sunny's voice was low and strong. Her teary lyrics told the stories earnestly, tortured, twisted, and personal. Agile fingers fluttered over the neck of her scuffed black fender. Her renditions yanked the heartstrings while the sax tore holes in their souls. Overtaken by the Blues, fans hollered and banged their hands together, drank, and danced until they dripped sweat.

Sunny wasn't black, surprising many fans who had only heard her recordings. Her old torch-style singing struck folks deeply. Local music critics seemed disappointed that she was a tall, blond, mullet sporting creature, heavy set and southern. It was harder to sell a gritty, buxom woman, dressing in tailored suits and butch to the nines. But she showed the spark of a star. She had the drawing power, was glamorous, and was comfortable in dingy bars because she had grown up in them. Her mother had been a singer. Music was in her blood.

When the press asked her, she swore that losing everything at fourteen forged her style. She would recall the feeling of determination and anger that plotted her destiny. Stories in music rags reported her mother as an entertainer turned addict that was overwhelmed early, becoming frazzled, fading, and finally succumbing to heroin. She died at thirty, leaving Sunny heartbroken and abandoned.

"Yes, I'm bitter. Bitter about being left behind. Mom suffered. She always seemed to suffer. Everything seemed dark. Depression is like that. I loved her. She tried. She gave me my start," she told the press. "It's lonely being free, right? Maybe that's why I reach out with music, a bridge to someone somewhere?" she smiled broadly. "It is sad if the applause is the only thing that warms ya. I'm lucky. I'm in love, and I love to sing. I keep it simple and let Kelly negotiate," she checked her watch. "Some say the glass is half full. Some say half empty. I think it's just another trick question."

Tonight, the volume was turned up exactly right. It filled the spaces in Oceanna's head, leaving little room for thought or conversation. Encouraging close cheeks, cuddling up, and talking directly into each other's ears.

But there were gaps and a couple of short breaks allowing Viv to work on her sales pitch. She was generous with the drinks and strategic with the compliments she aimed. When she needed leverage, she tried to consult Oceanna, pulling her in for confirmation. She nodded and shrugged uncomfortably.

"You are beautiful, Kelly. I think I have the skill and colors to bring it out, giving you an enhanced professional look. That can mean more opportunities. More doors open," Viv was getting touchy; the drinks were loosening them both.

"We're doing it ourselves now. Doors are already opening. We sell the music. Do we really need a fixer?" Kelly brought a cigarette to her lips, and Viv quickly lit it.

"But, you're growing and getting bigger. When you get to Hollywood, you're going to need a look. It's gonna matter. Just let me do your makeup and hair for some gigs."

Kelly interrupted, "Who told you about Hollywood?"

". . . your drummer, anyway, just some remodeling, like curb appeal for Anna's antique house. It's an eye sore now but with a little work . . ." Leaning forward, Viv's blouse fell open a bit more. "If you give me a chance, I'll prove it to you."

Popping a glance at Oceanna, Kelly asked, "Criteria for your success will be an increase for the band in what way, Viv? More rave reviews? We get them now. More drooling fans? More pretty women are hanging around. Starstruck young wannabes? Grabbing at my wife? Maybe you think a new comb-over will do the trick, Viv, and maybe you are willing to do more than head hair to get into show business," two shots of brandy went down fast.

A sax riff came to a scorching climax, blocking Oceanna from overhearing for a Moment.

She was grateful. Viv was leaning in too close to Kelly, nearly getting a shot glass in the eye as Kelly tossed another one back.

"Getting close to musicians hasn't hurt your business career either," said Viv. They looked at each other, up close, in the eye. "Don't let crow's feet cause creeping insecurity or block you. Give me a chance. Think about it. I'll do a great job on your comb-over for free!" she smiled.

Life at fifty was a curse and a blessing, depending on women in show business. Feminism and fortitude framed and freed Kelly, an artist in her own right and now a contract negotiator. The ware and tare and late nights were showing. She had been slugging it out for ten years in music with Sunny. It was fun but brutal at times, and she felt it. She was the stopgap, the rope that bound them, comforted them, and stood up against storms. The cold years of trial and error were behind her. She had brought them to the brink of recognition. Now a hissing snake had ensnared her. She was confident about her smarts but worried about the deepening lines.

Ashamed that she hadn't moved past the old double standards. She felt the impact of Viv's insolent pitch. Entirely gray, she felt old. Refusing to change the color and knowing brains bested beauty, she admitted she had considered plastic surgery privately. Sunny was ten years younger, and Kelly looked at least ten years older, at least.

From across the table, Oceanna could almost see steam shooting out of Kelly's nostrils. Boiling but restrained. The conversation quieted. They stared into each other's faces, breathing. Bracing for a fight, Oceanna leaned back, choosing to let them have it out, learn a lesson, no interference. Who would start it with a slap? Punch? Strangle? A drink in the face?

She sat on the edge of the stool and slid her smokes into her pocket in case they had to run. Things seemed to be moving in slow motion. Symbols crashed, drums throbbed, and the last song was sung. Standing applause. Sunny bowed. The crowd yelled for more. Kelly and Viv stared at each other, then turned to look at Oceanna, frozen.

Kelly stood and said, "I'll call ya." Winking at Oceanna, she wove her way to Sunny at center stage to discuss the encore.

C H A P T E R 1 1 :

"DREAM," THE BLUE-RIBBON MARE.

Counting the squares on the calendar backwards, she calculated the days until her birthday, as she had done with anticipation every year. She crossed April's clean white squares off with a red pen with relish.

Maria hummed at the glistening black mare in the rodeo poster, galloping over the green grass, mane fluttering, pink nostrils flaring, kicking up her heels, reading, "Dream," The Blue-Ribbon Mare. Kentucky, USA."

Dream had come to life in Maria's mind after she had salvaged the poster from behind the bleachers at a rodeo she had gone to with her father. He rode the bulls, and she oiled the gear and kept the camper safe. She had fallen in love with the grace and powerful look of the perfect horse. Dream had become an imaginary best friend.

She would imagine Dream's black coat hot in the sun, rippling muscles shivering under it. Conjuring a perfect day, she could feel her palms rolling over her back, bathing her, washing off the dust of the ride, feeling the strength of her body. Laying her head on her pillow at night, she imagined it was Dream's side, rippling with the rhythm of the rise and fall breaths. Maria pressed herself into her ribs, rocking to a hero's heartbeat.

Playing outside alone, she conjured up a bareback ride, feeling the thud of hooves ringing through her bones. Kids made fun of her for pretending her to gallop and talking to herself. Little girls thought she was weird and ran home. Being small and skinny, she avoided the boys.

When being alone frightened her, she recalled a bright western carnival with rows of red, white, and blue flags stuck to circles of rail fences and the sneer of the bucking bulls her father would attempt to ride. The rough riders daring to try to stay on, limbs flapping, flailing, and being thrown into the air. Brave contenders are being ground into the dirt by a ton of hoof and horn but living to tell. The rescue clowns rushing in to draw them away. The smell of hay and leather gave her peace. Cheers from the crowd thrilled her. The sea of tall western hats on the crowd of heads in the bleachers and big belt buckles flashing in the sun brightened her. Hotdogs with chili dripping and a beer, if she could sneak it, made her laugh.

Her own boots were red ostrich skin. Her belt, made in Mexico, was carved with her name. The large buckle, polished and proudly worn with her jeans, proudly she would ride Dream. She envisioned galloping through lush green meadows high on the thrill.

Maria's escape was daily. When she woke for school, instead of waking to a house with her father snoring off a hangover on the couch, she pretended to brush the hay from her long black hair, having dreamt of sleeping in the stall with Dream as her pillow. Resting to a dream of the rustle of doves cooing as they nested, her lullaby, the moan of horse breaths.

Uncomfortable in school dresses that had to be kept clean, she wore tee shirts and jeans with cuffs and a red vest with white fringe that matched her boots. She imagined herself with a broad-brimmed hat, chaps, and six guns buckled around her tiny waist. She smoked tobacco while contemplating the sky at night and sometimes chewed a matchstick.

Finding children her own age lacking in bravery and imagination, she galloped alone around the playground, grudgingly dismounting when she had to return to class. At recess, she would bring sugar cubes to Dream, waiting along the fences to settle her from pawing the ground impatiently. When her father was on the road, she spread beans on tortillas for dinner, imagining a campout under the stars on Bob's fold-out couch.

If school was in session and she had to stay home, she readied the house for his return. When her father dragged in, exhausted from the long days caring for horses or from days away at the rodeo trying for prize money, she would get lost in the stories. Ralfie told of his adventures while she put ice on his bruises.

She would brush and braid his long black hair into two pigtails down each side of his head. He told her it was the tradition of their people. So, she did the same. Trying to be like her father was tricky. He walked straight back and limped with bowed legs. Short and lean, he practically disappeared when he turned sideways. His arms were long and powerful. His dark, rough hands were skillful. But they naturally shared the charm of a similar, broad white smile and a ridiculous sense of humor they loved to show off, whether others appreciated it or not.

"Dream, let's have a birthday party! Hotdogs and chili and a chocolate cake, with nine candles." She pets the soft muzzle as Dream blew breath into Maria's face. "We need to plan this thing, horsy, right?" She pulled out an old shopping list and wrote the plans on the back.

"We have to invite Bob and his mom, of course. And what about the new ladies? Let's have it there, in the backyard, with a barbecue. Right?" Dream fluttered her lips and pulled a pigtail. "This means we need money. Some good money to buy this. We need a J-O-B, horsey! J-O-B." She looked at the calendar and then the wall clock. "It's time for the breakfast, and Bob's got the cakes!"

Unfolding her long legs, Dream stood and shook her flanks.

"Okay, I need to get my pants on." Yanking on her jeans, she dropped to the floor, pulled on white socks and boots, and folded her pant cuffs. She checked the shine of the secret boot knife, wiped it with her bandana, and located it back onto the hidden sheath along her calf. Treading her belt through the loops, she made sure the oval buckle was front and center. With her red kerchief, she polished the buckle and stuffed it in her rear pocket. After checking her leather wallet for any cash, she repeated herself.

"We need a job. Badly." Dream pawed the floor, reminding Maria the pancakes at Bob's would be waiting. Bob's house was only ten doors down. They could gallop there in a minute. She pets the only white on Dream's body, the white star on her forehead, then grabbed a fist full of main, swung her legs up and around her, and withers to a solid fit onto her back. She shivered. They jumped out the door, trotted down the stairs from the porch to the sidewalk, and carefully hesitated to look at Oceanna's house across the street.

"We could do a lot of work for them. We could start with the garden; pulling the weeds would be worth a twenty at least," she said to herself. Dream kept dancing in place, fighting her desire to run. Maria clucked and gave a little heel, and they were off.

Galloping down the sidewalk, Dream placed her hooves over the cracks and curbs as they went. The ride was smooth and easy. Dream shook her head and slid to a stop in front of Bob's picket fence. They could smell the cooking from the street. Bob fried it with butter.

C H A P T E R   1 2 :

OFFICER CAKE

"Humm . . . looks like the rear leg is fractured." Maria poked at the stiff grey limb sticking out of the drain grate in the middle of the street. "This opossum had big car trouble, right Dreamer?"

Dream shook her head and fluttered her long black eyelashes. Pulling out a small spiral notebook and a short pencil, she scribbled her findings.

"Opossum dead, found at 17th and Alder. Leg broken, messed up toenails, death by car. Flat and stiff. Smell rotten. No worms." She drew a rough sketch of the body and closed the notebook with a snap. A veterinarian trainee's work was never done.

"Okay. It's official. That's the third one today. One squirrel, one racoon, and now this." She wrapped her arms around Dream's neck and felt comforted by her soft heat. It scared her to see road-kill. They had galloped many blocks away from home, and her feet ached, clomping like horse hooves wore down the heels after a mile or so. She pulled her red kerchief from her back pocket, wiped the sweat from her face, and tied it around her neck, cowgirl style. Then started to backtrack through the neighborhoods of southeast Portland.

She took the winding route that passed by several old grandmothers that often sat on their porches or tended rose beds. If Maria found them in their gardens, they might be willing to chat and offer her a chair, a cookie, and water. They were familiar with Maria and Dream.

Grandmotherly instincts drew them to her, watching her trot past, clucking, and talking to her horse, dressed like a pioneer in the wild west, sweating alone. They offered her water and listened to her stories about her father at rodeos, riding bulls, and how she followed the trauma doctors, stopping the bleeding if there were an injured competitor.

One old lady who had been a nurse in the war gave her guidance on how to pack her first aid kits she took to the events, just in case, and gave her a slender book on first aid. They discussed how to back a belly wound and splint a leg using sticks and towels. Maria looked at the anatomy pictures and drew her own versions in her notebook for when she got home.

One lady was a baker and traded her fresh bread in exchange for Maria's recipes for Mexican dishes, including the secrets for making thick tortillas filled with flavorful beans and spicey tamales.

"Dream, and I found three carcasses today," she said. "The critters are very fast! The cars go too fast if they can beat a squirrel."

"You didn't see a large tiger-striped cat, did you?" One grandmother asked.

"No. Did it have a collar? Where does it live?"

"I couldn't see a collar, but It's very large. A Maine Coon cat!" The grandmother leaned in close to Maria's face. "It's a giant! Over three feet long. It jumped off my porch and ran down the street when I was watering the roses. I almost fainted. I hope you can save that one." she took a sip of the tea.

"Wow! We are going to look for that cat! We've got to go, grandmother. Thanks for the cookies." Maria folded several more cookies into a napkin and stuffed them into her vest pocket. Even smashed, the crumbs of her pastries were tasty. She mounted and clomped down the wooden stairs to the sidewalk and galloped off in the direction of home.

"Be careful with the tiger. It's as big as you are!" She yelled to Maria before she disappeared, bouncing behind the Lilacs, galloping five blocks before slowing to a trot.

"Dream, we are on a mission now, a real mission to save the lost cat. We have to be smart when on patrol." With a whinny, they turned the corner, and Bob's house came into view.

He was on the porch swing, moving slowly back and forth with his eyes closed, humming to himself softly. His thin lips moving, wordlessly. He did not acknowledge Maria as she trotted to his crooked picket fence, leaned on the gate, and watched him, not breaking the trance.

The smooth roll of the swing drifted him to a place in the past where comfort met conflict. Bob did not fight the torment or judge the tormentor. He felt involved and connected. Nurse Ambrosia cared that he was there in her own special way.

Her smoker's voice was raspy.

"Selfish little Bobby! Do not deny it. You are not a polite guy!" The night guard looked toward the loud voices and stood up from his stool down the hall.

"I've got this! I'll let you know if I need you, darling", she waved him back. He winked and returned to his stool and magazine. "I will have to teach you a lesson. Right?"

Bob stood still and blinked several times in agreement. At thirteen, he was taller than she. He looked down at her faded red lace bra and pale cleavage. After she had bathed several patience, he could smell her talcum powder and sweat.

"You are a nasty boy! Looking at me like that will get you in trouble!" She slipped a small bottle of vodka from her dingy uniform pocket deep into the front of his pants.

"Be sure your closet is clean, mister, and I will be checking later tonight," she took hold of his arm.

He could feel her breasts against him as she turned him toward his door. He began to blush. Hiding in the closet became a sanctuary and a passion. He missed her even after many years.

Watching him hum and peep with his eyes pinched shut, Maria leaned in. She tried to make the sounds he was making and wondered what they meant. Bob was often complicated and paradoxical but always good to her. With Bob as a friend, she could forget about the bullies. In exchange, she did the thinking for both. Fixing her eyes tightly on Bob, she did not notice the car slowly pulling up behind.

Officer Emerald Cake sat silently observing the peculiar sight. The cruiser purred. Her German Sheppard K-9, Zsa-Zsa, panted and stared, twitching her black nose, sniffing the air from the back seat. She huffed and gave a low growl, rattling up from her belly. Cake hushed her with a hand gesture. Zsa-Zsa drooled motionlessly, nose pressed to the mesh screen over the open widow.

Maria began to rock gently to the rhythm Bob made. Like matching metronomes in even movements. Right, left, right, left. Cake and Zsa-Zsa s eyes rolled back and forth in their sockets as they watched their somber dance. Then, at the far end of Bob's neglected yard, parting the long weed grasses, dandelions, and thorns, a fat orange face peered out.

Zsa-Zsa saw her first, froze, and stared. The cat stepped out, all three feet of her, with shaggy paws and yellow striped legs and tail. The dog panted and drooled. Her nose shoved into the screen. Striding along the side of the cruiser, she passed under the rear window, bobbing her long tail just under the dog's nose.

Zsa-Zsa lunged hard and barked viciously, rocking the cruiser and shocking Cake. She swung her head forward, lurching her face against the steering wheel, hitting her horn. The sudden blast of the horn alarmed Maria, causing her to spin her head, surprising her to see the police car close behind and a huge ball of fur jumping the fence in a single leap, directly over her head, squalling. Maria ducked the cat, fell to her knees, and fainted.

CHAPTER 13:

THE GIANT

"**D**amn it Zsa-Zsa! Stay!" Cake thrust opens the cruiser's heavy door and unfolded her legs, ducked the frame, and rushed out. Zsa-Zsa panted and drooled in silence, waiting for her door to open and the leash to be snapped on, her brown eyes glinting with excitement.

Kneeling at the crumpled heap that was Maria, Cake felt her pulse and pet her head. She had seen her drop and gently laid her flat on the sidewalk with her jacket under her head.

"Are you alright? Can you hear me?" She spoke into Maria's face and assessed her for any abrasions or blood. Maria started to stir. Coughing softly, her hands clutched Cake's arm.

"What happened?" She opened her eyes and wondered if she was in trouble, seeing the flash of a badge. "What did I do? What did I do?" She kicked her feet a few times as a show of strength and struggled to sit up, leaning against the fence.

"You fainted. It looks like we startled you." Cake removed her sunglasses and continued to check for damage. "Are you alright?" She smiled and brushed the sand off Maria's vest. "I'm Officer Emerald

Cake, and that is K-9 Officer Zsa-Zsa, my partner." Pointing at Zsa-Zsa, pressing her nose against the screen, she asked. "Can I let her out? She wants to meet you."

"Oh yes! Let me see her," she forgot her sore elbows.

"Here, let me help you. You may not be steady."

Maria gazed into the gentle bronze face and found herself captivated by Cake's large green eyes and wide white smile. Maria watched as Cake rose to her full height, at an altitude of six foot, eight inches in stalking feet. Six foot ten, in boots. Maria gazed up, disoriented.

"Holey beans. Is this happening?" she grinned, shuffled carefully over to the back door of the car, and held her palm out, prepared to meet Zsa-Zsa.

Cake gave the command to stay, opened the door, and snapped on the leash, then gave the signal to come out and meet a friend, and the dog jumped down.

As soon as the big black nose met Maria's scrapped hand, tails wagged, and Maria cried.

"Oh, she is beautiful. What a good girl!" Rubbing her cheeks and whiskers, Zsa-Zsa relaxed and sat.

"Oh, can I play with her sometime?" Maria asked. Kneeling down, she let Zsa-Zsa lick her face.

"Well, it looks like you are already friends, but Zsa-Zsa is a professional officer dog, so let's go slow and get to know each other for a while, Okay?"

"Oh, that's great!" Maria sniffled. "Can we really be friends?" She leaned her head way back to look at the expression on Cake's face to see if she meant it.

"Oh ya. And I wonder if you could help us find a bad guy. Is this your house?"

"No. I live about down there." She pointed down the street. "Me and my Father live across from the haunted house. You know, the old house looks like a witch house, with a tower and some new ladies living there."

"So, who is in this house? And who is that man, your friend?" Cake and Maria turned to watch for a moment. Bob, still mumbling and rolling on his swing, undistracted.

"That is my best friend, Bob Smack. His mom says he is a paradox. Dolly is his mom, and they live here. They watch over me when my father is at the rodeo, riding bulls and helping with stuff there, all over. If it is school time, I stay home, and they help me. My father takes the pull-behind camper to the fairs, and if it is summer, I go and take care of the gear and sleep in the trailer. I don't ride in the rodeo, but I follow the doctors around and watch the first aid and learn to be a Vet someday." Maria panted and smiled. Zsa-Zsa sniffed the air in Bob's direction.

"That's why you dress like a Cowgirl. I see. Is your father home now?"

"No. He's shoeing horses this week, but he should be home tomorrow. I will make the dinner of steak and potatoes for him and help put away the gear and stuff." She sat on the ground and scratched Zsa-Zsa s head.

"Wow. He is lucky to have a daughter like you," Cake continued to look at Bob. "Is his mom home now?"

"Oh, ya. Dolly stays inside most of the time. She is nice but very white and kind of sick or something. She has long gray hair, like she is old, but her face is kind of young looking and pretty. It's weird, but she is nice."

"How does she take care of you then.?" Said Cake.

"Well, Bob plays with me, and she does the cooking. She is a very good cook, and she makes flapjacks. That's pancakes with lots of butter and syrup," her stomach growled. "I could eat some now. I am getting to be friends with the new ladies too, so they can help take care of me as well, and I want them to pay me to help fix up the garden because I want to have twenty bucks and have a party there for my birthday." Maria took a breath. "Could you come and bring your dog?"

"I will consider it. Ahhh, what is your name, cowgirl?"

"I'm Maria Brava, which means brave Maria."

"Okay, that's good because I need help catching a bad guy."

"Oh, yes, we can help," said Maria as she smoothed Zsa-Zsa s ears.

Who's "we"? asked Cake.

"I play that I have a horse named Dream, that I ride all around the neighborhood checking for hurt animals. She is an all-black mare. Some kids think it's weird to play like that, but it makes me feel good to have someone to talk to. Bob doesn't talk much, but he understands," she pulled out her spiral notebook and showed Cake the list of animals she documented, including place, description, and cadaver sketches.

Cake looked closely at the details in the notebook and unfolded several sheets of paper from her own pocket.

"I think I found the right person for the job, Maria. Look at these pictures of these girls. Do you know them? They are about your age. Maybe you go to their school?" Maria looked closely, tracing the pictures with her finger.

"Nope, I don't know them. I don't play with other kids because they think I'm weird. I play with Bob. Kids think he is weird, and I talk to myself, and they scare me," she started to tear up.

"Okay, Maria Brava, I need your help to watch for suspicious activity. There is someone taking girls, kidnapping them. You know what I mean?" Cake knelt down to her level and wiped her tears. "It's alright to be scared sometimes. Now you have two new friends, me and Zsa-Zsa, and I want to make you a deputy. We are going to be patrolling all around here to keep looking for the bad guy. The more people we have looking out, the sooner he will be caught. Right?"

"Right!" She sniffed and continued to look at the pictures in her hand.

Cake removed a small police pin from her shirt and snapped it onto Maria's vest.

The police radio started to make scratchy sounds, and a dispatcher started to call out codes. Zsa-Zsa stood up at attention.

"Maria, I've got to go, but I'll be back. Tell Bob and his mother and your father I'm going to come and talk to all the neighbors about this. Here is my card with my phone number. Call if you see anything." Quickly, Zsa-Zsa jumped back into the cruiser. Cake started to fold herself back into the rig. "Be very careful, Maria. I'll be back soon. Call me. We are partners now!" She slammed the door and turned on the lights and pulled out down the street.

Maria stood stunned and delighted, watching the car disappear. She looked again at the pictures of the girls in one scraped hand and then at Cake's police card in the other and touched the embossed official emblem in gold, then peeked at the small, pinned badge on her vest.

"Wow, Dream! We know a giant!" she sighed.

CHAPTER 14:

WHO IS AFRAID OF DOLLY SMACK?

The next day Officer Cake pulled up in front of Bob's house, retrieved Zsa-Zsa from the back seat, and both stood and looked. Zsa-Zsa, pop-eyed and panting, sniffed for the cat. She could tell it had been hanging around in the grass. If she was lucky, she may still be sleeping under the overgrown Camellia bushes or just leaving a trail of tufts of orange fir behind that could be easily followed.

Cake took inventory. Paint peeling and wood rotting, weeds tangling the old roses, and un-mowed grass exposed Bob and Dolly were not gardeners. The place wasn't trashy, just neglected, thought Cake. If Bob and Dolly were both disabled, maybe they were home much of the time and could have seen something suspicious. How sick was Dolly, she wondered? Bob looked almost comatose the day before. What could the inside be like? She shuddered.

Cake knocked softly on the stained-glass panel in the middle of the front door several times. She called out.

"Hello, this is Officer Emerald Cake of the Portland Police making a wellness call. Are you alright?" Zsa-Zsa panted quietly, staring at the doorknob she anticipated would soon shake.

Through the glass, movement could be seen. They waited, considering it may take time for Dolly to respond. Was she in a wheelchair? Zsa-Zsa sniffed at the door frame. A figure appeared behind the glass, and several deadbolts clacked as they were unlatched, and the door was pulled open. Bob's grinning face appeared.

"Hi," he said in a fragile high voice, not matching his thick stature. He fluttered his eyelids.

"Hi. Are you Bob, Maria's friend?" She removed her sunglasses and smiled back. "Bob, I am Officer Cake, and this is my K-9 officer. I wonder, if your mother is home, could I talk to you both about an important matter?"

"Mom! Cops, Mom!" he giggled and yelled into the room behind him.

"Let them in, Bobby! Please, honey. Bring them to me," a soft but authoritative voice called back.

Bob swung the door open wide, and Cake and Zsa-Zsa stepped into the dark room, letting their eyes adjust for a moment. As the shadows gave way to form and color, Cake observed a small pale figure reclining on a couch, looking up at her, and smelled perfume. The room was hot.

Dolly slowly sat up to greet the officer, who, with one long step, had landed in the middle of her living room. Her eyes traced the broad shoulders looming above her. Her pristine uniform fitting well to her long frame, with her blue tie and bright badge. Dolly could not help but smile back at the large bright green eyes and wide welcoming expression, including dimpled cheeks. She felt a flutter.

"Well! I'll be damned! They have much improved their standards at the department, Officer. Even the K-9s are more beautiful." Her voice was breathy. She laughed and leaned forward to extend her hand.

Zsa-Zsa was signaled to sit as Cake reached out to take her hand. Dolly's fingers were small and cool as they landed in her own rugged palms. She was careful not to squeeze too hard but shook with an official firmness and gentle reassurance. She assessed the nature of the small woman before her, her gray hair laying over her narrow-exposed shoulders and pale skin, spooky, as Maria had described. Her smooth cheeks only hinted at her age, with faint wrinkles around her pale blue eyes, full lips with coral lipstick, highlighted with light brown mascara, carefully applied, as though Cake had been expected.

Her nightgown was purple and silky. Around her shoulders was a gauzy shawl that floated like a cloud to her feet, which were bare, white, and well-manicured. Cake felt a pang of sadness and a bit sick, intruding on her, bearing witness to her fading glamour.

"Close the door, Bobby, honey, and let's talk to Office Cake. Come on and sit with me, Officer." She patted the cushion next to her, gracefully swinging her feet under her hips to make room. "Would you care for a smoke?" she asked as she tapped a menthol out of the pack for herself.

"Yes, thank you," Cake said, surprised at her sudden need for a smoke. Quitting had been a challenge. She carefully took a seat, arranged her belt and holster, tucked her knees between the couch and the glass coffee table, and took one.

Dolly took close notice of her guest as she leaned closer to give her a light. Bob closed the door and sat in a recliner at the other end of the couch, wringing his hands. Cake figured the recliner was Bob's favorite spot. It fit him like a glove.

"So, what's going on?" Dolly said as she blew out a cloud of smoke. "Is this just a wellness check?"

"No. I did talk to Bob's friend, Maria. She informed me you take care of her when her father is off working at rodeos."

"Right, Maria is a great kid. Very cute, pretending to ride her horse around the sidewalks. We have her in and feed her. Bob is her hero. They spend lots of time together, here or at her house. He is very protective. Right honey?"

He smiled wide and put his thick hand over his heart. "Right Mom."

"Well, we have a possible kidnapper in the area, and I'm concerned. Here are the pictures of two kids that are missing. Do you know them, or have you seen them? As far as we can tell, they were taken off the streets while going to school on foot. Maria is at risk of abduction." Cake handed the pictures to Dolly, and she passed them to Bob.

"I haven't seen them. I hardly leave the house, as you can probably see. Bob may have seen something." She leaned over the arm of the couch, picked up the ashtray, and offered it to Cake. She flicked the ash. "My Bobby tends to intimidate others. If she is with Bob, no one would dare to hurt her."

"Is he always around?" Cake watched her expression for any hints of deception. Why was Dolly housebound? Was she mentally or physically compromised?

She scanned the room discreetly now that her eyes had adjusted to the dimness. The room had a strange stale atmosphere. Sad. Depressed. The fireplace mantle had framed pictures. One of a policeman. Several of a glamorous actress, several costumes, all of them dramatic, maybe Dolly.

"No, that's right, he goes to the workshop for the disabled three days a week. He sorts things for the thrift shops. He loves it. Lots of friends he made when he was in the sanitorium work there too. The lift driver is even one of the old nurses or something from there. She comes right in front and beeps instead of making Bob stand outside and wait. She's an older gal, kind of odd but friendly. She drives all around, picking up people. She may know something. She's picking Bob up today at 9:30. You could meet her in about fifteen minutes." She patted Bob's hand. "Are you ready?"

Pulling out a small notebook Cake wrote down Dolly's information and her own observations. "What's her name? Do you know? Could you tell me about the sanatorium? Why was Bob there?"

"Hang on, officer, I need a drink if we are going down that ugly rabbit hole," she tapped Bob's knee. "Bob, could you make us a drink, baby, really quick? Before the bus comes. Bring the cart," smiling at Cake, she assured her. "I know you are on duty, officer; Bob's dad was a cop; he downed a few drinks while on duty. That's for another day. But you can have a martini when you come back . . . for another "wellness check," Okay?" She winked and patted Cake's knee. "You will come and check again, won't you?"

"Yes," she said nervously. Cake gave her a once over, visually examining Dolly's face and form. Noticing her casual flirtatious body language, showy lingerie, and penetrating glances. She noticed Dolly scanning her, then looking directly into her eyes for confirmation. Protected by her crisp uniform, badge, and belts, she typically felt safe and neutral. But Dolly seemed to be encouraged by it. Attracted to armor, she noted.

Bob returned from the kitchen with a narrow tea cart set up as a rolling bar, with an ice bucket and glasses and a bottle of Vodka in the ice. He poured the drink quickly and delivered it to Dolly's side table, crowded with pill bottles. She plucked a couple of pink pills from one of the bottles, popped them into her mouth, and drank the martini down gracefully.

Bob went to the window and looked out at the street anxiously. The clock on the side table peeped. "Time, Mom!" he said, hurrying to the coat rack. He pulled on a large, hooded canvas coat.

Cake noted his agility as he pulled on the coat and grabbed his lunch box. He stood rocking from one foot to the other, facing the street, ready for his ride.

"Your shoes are untied, Bobby! Can you help him, officer? He can do so many things except talk and tie his shoes," she smiled.

Cake was thankful to unfold her legs and kneel down to help Bob's shoes. Shoe size and make notes. Zsa-Zsa sat up and licked her lips.

Watching her partner closely. A special needs transport shuttle pulled up next to the curb and beeped her horn. Bob said thanks and pulled open the door, trotted down the stairs, and into the shuttle. Cake focused on the driver's face, hair color and age, license plate number and was going to go down and question her when the dispatcher began to squeak, and the bus pulled away.

"Duty calls, right?" said Dolly pouring herself another drink.

"Right. Thanks for the help. Be careful. Here is my card. Call me if you have any information," she spoke firmly and then softened. "Keep an eye out, and we'll be back. We are patrolling around here often if you need us."

"When you come back, we can talk, and I'll share some of the family history. Get to know each other better?" She smiled and started to look a bit dreamy-eyed.

Zsa-Zsa followed Cake to the front door. Looking back at Dolly, she felt sick and sad, feeling both repulsed and attracted. Shaking her head, she pulled closed the door. Dolly waved goodbye with the business card between her fingers.

They moved to the cruiser. Cake felt compelled to look back before getting behind the wheel at the dilapidated home. Still standing but neglected. She felt an uncomfortable flutter and denied it to herself.

"Zsa-Zsa, we have our work cut out for us, babe," dog growled softly and jumped in.

CHAPTER 15:

SEX TOYS

Gripping the bathrobe around her and dragging the terry cloth belt, she descended the narrow staircase in a rush. The knock on the door was a pound, and a cop car was parked in the driveway. Oceanna spun the deadbolts and yanked the door open, flustered and panting, then paused. Surprised at the size of the woman before her, she felt small and in need of reassurance. She had to look up to read the name tag on her chest and felt trapped in the piercing eyes of her large, alert German Shepard sitting at attention at her side.

"Oh, g-g-good morning, Officer e-e-Emerald Cake." She stuttered and exerted a friendly smile.

"Good morning. As you have noticed, I am Officer Emerald Cake, and this is my K-9 partner, Zsa-Zsa. We are investigating a call about a suspicious person last night. Lurking around the hedges? Are you the homeowner, Oceanna Pontiac?"

"Oh good, yes, I saw someone in the backyard."

Cake scribbled in her notebook. "Your name is spelled like the Indian tribe, Pontiac?"

"Yah, like the old car maker."

She grinned and noted Oceanna's short mussy blond hair and brown eyes. "Are you a member of a tribe?"

"No," she said. "But I am a fan of old cars. Great hood ornamentations. I miss that."

"Are you a car buff? I noticed the tail end of what looks like a '60s model in the driveway."

"Oh. That is my '67 Dart, with original gold paint. I do all the work on it. Best car I have ever owned."

Cake noted her eyes flashing with pride and removed her sunglasses to look directly at her.

"Can you give a description of your peeper?"

"Well . . . it was dark, and the back porch light is out. He looked fat-ish, wearing a heavy coat with a hood. I'm not sure of the color, but sort of tan, I guess. He scooted away when I opened the door. I was taking out the trash to the cans in the backyard. He looked hunched over and tip-toed away," she shrugged apologetically. "I yelled at him to leave us alone."

Oceanna felt exposed by Cake's x-ray green eyes. Her cheeks reddened. With nowhere to hide, she pulled the robe closer and tied the belt tighter.

"I'm patrolling the streets looking for two girls that have gone missing. You may have seen the flyers?" Cake pulled out a flyer with pictures of the missing girls, descriptions, and where they were last seen. Oceanna nodded as she looked over the details.

"The guy that's lurking around may be the same one that's taking the kids."

"Yes, I got one of these in my mailbox. I don't know them. We just moved in here about a month ago. This is terrifying," she frowned.

"In March? That's when the first girl disappeared. You know Maria Brava that lives across the street?" Cake pointed over her shoulder to the yellow house directly across the narrow street, with a polished red and white camper trailer in the driveway.

"Oh, yah. Little Maria is our new friend. She and Bob Smack, the disabled man that lives down the street, have a clubhouse in the basement. They're helping fix up the house. Painting and doing some gardening. I pay them for their help. We're friends now. Viv and I watch over her when her father is working out of town with horses and riding in rodeos. Summer's coming, and he said she may need looking after due to his being gone often."

"Right. I've met Bob and his mother. She helps with Maria too, right? I'm worried about her imaginary galloping around alone. She's small and vulnerable."

"She said she wears a knife in her boot. But I get your point," Oceanna smiled shyly.

Zsa-Zsa barked and stood suddenly. Oceanna flinched. Cake reached over Oceanna's head, pushed the door open further, and whiffed smoke coming from the interior of the house.

"Is something burning inside?" said Cake extending a long arm over Oceanna's head to hold open the door.

"O-o-oh, well . . . that's my partner, Viv, she's doing . . . some kind of . . . cleansing . . ." Surprised, she stepped back, her heart pounded.

"Smells herbal. Are you smoking something illegal?" Cake noticed smoke gathering around the ceiling coming down the stairs. A woman screamed. She pushed past Oceanna and rushed into the hall. Zsa-Zsa pulling at the leash, and they headed up the curved staircase, her shoulders brushing the walls, Zsa-Zsa's toenails clattering on the wooden steps.

Charging up, three steps at a time, up two flights of stairs, Cake and dog reached the door of the turret in a flash. Sliding open the ornate door, dense smoke filled the staircase. Tall flames fluttered from a large bowl on a table in the middle of the room where a woman was waving her hands, trying to put it out.

Two women on a black velvet couch screamed in shock and recoiled. In one long step, Cake pushed herself between the fire and the flustered woman, took off her jacket, threw it over the fire, and smothered the flames. Oceanna cranked opened several windows to let out the smoke. For a moment, they were silent, panting.

Looking around the room as the smoke cleared and the danger was over, Cake stood to her full height, catching a delicate hanging mobile made of oak leaves and twigs in her short, tousled hair. Her jacket was soaked and smoldering in a pool of sage and rosemary water in a bowl on a round table in the middle of the room.

Vivian stood in her kimono, sleeves singed, with a black leather harness around her hips, housing a bright red phallus protruding from it. The women on the couch laid back on top of each other, mouths agape, staring up at the heroic Amazon.

Cake eyed the situation. The women were shocked but smiling. Viv, with her long dark braided hair with her phallus, bare-chested and burnt. The smell of the roasting herbs on the table with a pentagram in lay, round walls, and the view of the neighborhood from the convex windows of the tower room, venting smoke. She told Zsa-Zsa to sit. She sat and wagged her tail.

Pulling out the small notebook, she began to scribble impatiently.

"Magic spell?" she stared at Viv.

"No, Ma'am."

"Witchcraft?" She pointed with her pencil to the volumes of books around the walls of Astrology, Tarot, and Herbal Healing.

"No, Ma'am." Said Viv.

"Arson?" She grinned.

"Well, I was heating up the room, Officer." She turned to face Cake and flung opened her robe, showing her bare breasts with her hands on her hips and waggling the red rubber erection.

Cake looked at the spectacle, up and down, and backed up again, slowly.

"I see," she said. "Sex worker?"

"Are you gonna cuff her?" Popped up one of the couch ladies eagerly.

Viv stomped her bare foot.

"No, Ma'am! I am an entrepreneur. I was burning a sage bundle to set the mood." She backed up to reveal a second table full of flavored lubricants, sex toys in various colors, and harnesses in a variety of materials and sizes for any woman. Viv waved her hand over the display with theatrical flair, displaying her products in a formal presentation.

"Set the mood for what, exactly?"

"These women are my customers! They are being fitted," said Viv.

The ladies giggled, and Oceanna dropped her face in her hands.

"I do product parties for women that want a proper fitting toy and instructions on how to use them. There is skill involved in their use, you know." She picked up one of her business cards and handed it to Cake.

"CozmetixX? Vivian Lash? That's you?"

"Yes, I sell only high-quality products, and I do creative makeovers. If you are ever interested, I'll give you a deal," she smiled and winked.

"I see. Thank you." Cake nodded, pulled out another small notebook, and handed it to the ladies on the couch.

"Names, addresses, and phones, please." She handed each of them a flyer of the lost children and asked them if they had seen the peeping-tom, gave them some facts, handed them each a card of her own, and told them she would be patrolling the area daily and to call if they saw anything.

Gathering Zsa-Zsa s leash, she smoothed her hair and turned to leave the room.

"Thank you, ladies, for the interesting time. Sorry I bothered you. Keep the jacket. And Ms. Lash? I think red is your color," she smiled. Viv curtsied.

"Ms. Pontiac? Will you show me out? I have another question."

She followed Oceanna, ducked the door frame, shut the door behind her, and led Zsa-Zsa down the stairs.

The ladies jumped up, beaming with joy, yelling, "Shit, Viv, your parties are better than Las Vegas!"

DETAILS

Oceanna tied her robe and slipped on moccasins before going onto the porch. Cake followed her onto the slightly leaning porch with turned pillars, gingerbread woodwork peeling several layers of paint, overgrown with lilac bushes full of rattling bees and a porch swing hanging from chains.

"What is it, officer?" Oceanna asked.

"Can we sit for a moment?" Cake arranged her belt and holster for comfort as she settled herself on the swing. Zsa-Zsa licked her nose and lay at her partner's feet, eyeing the bees.

Oceanna gazed at the long arm stretched across the back of the swing with a soft palm and long fingers, no rings, and perched herself next to Cake on the edge of her seat.

"Play Basketball?" asked Oceanna.

"Boxing," said Cake as she stretched out her free arm to it's full length, indicating the distance between herself and whoever was trying her. "They never touched me," she smiled broadly, flashing her teeth and dimples.

"My money's on you, Officer." Oceanna nodded and smiled back shyly.

"Listen, Ms. Pontiac."

"Uh, just call me Anna."

"Ok, just call me Cake." She continued to grin at Oceanna, who continued to blush. In an effort to imply some sense of confidence, she slid her hips back onto the seat and leaned against the swing back. She felt Cake's arm across her shoulders but pretended not to.

"This peeping-tom or whatever he is, could be extremely dangerous. He could be stalking or planning a break-in. This house may draw attention. How did you get ahold of this grand old Queen Ann?"

"My grandmother left it to me. There is no mortgage, and she left enough money to start fixing up the place, so I have time and money for now. I love the old houses. Are you a fan?"

"Oh ya. I studied architectural design in college before changing to Criminal justice. I wanted to build my own house with porches and turrets. I imagined having a bedroom in the tower with a glass dome ceiling. Just looking at the stars, out into the night," said Cake.

"Oh ya? What made you change your major."

"Justice. I figured while I was relatively young, very, very tall and strong, I could take the pressure and stand for what's right. There aren't enough black women on the police force," she grinned.

"Well, I do feel protected now that you are here," Oceanna shrugged nervously. "Both you and Zsa-Zsa."

Zsa-Zsa checked Oceanna, then stared back at the bees. She felt a bit dreamy listening to the buzzes floating on the smell of the lilacs.

"Give me a tour, and let's see what possible protection you can install."

They descended the stone stairs leading from the front door and porch to the brick path through the lawn, to the driveway, then to the backyard.

Oceanna pointed out the stairs and rough door to the basement clubhouse and told the story of her arrival, becoming overwhelmed by her grandmother's ghost and Bob and Maria.

Cake jotted down the hazards as they looked over the sideyard and backyard. Tangles of overgrown blackberries climbing the walls and stone chimney had injured the mortar and shingles and choked windows. Dense laurel hedges growing through a teetering fence and around the boundaries shaded the yard and offered lots of hiding places that would keep a prowler out of sight even during the day.

Ornate gingerbread carvings needed stripping and repainting. Wooden windows, after a century of loyal work, neglected for years, needed repair, and let in the cold. Throwing back their heads, they admired the turret above it, curved windows, boarded with stained glass, still venting smoke, topped with a pointed roof, and alive with small bats peeping and fluttering in their hidey-holes, in complaint.

"Even bats in your belfry. Wow, Anna, this place is a Zoo," Cake laughed. "Speaking of creatures, what is going on with Ms. Lash? I assume you are a couple."

"Oh ya, we are a couple. A couple of nuts."

"The relationship a bit strained?" pushed Cake.

"The relationship is passionate and fragile. Or maybe I'm just describing myself. Viv has ambitions. She was a successful makeup model but found it very tense, so she is trying to set up a "Personal Party Boutique" with whatever a woman needs. She is intent on establishing herself and making it a solid business, and as you saw, the demonstration is an important part of it. You have to admit, seeing her with the product makes a bold statement. I try to support her and keep out of the way."

"You spend your time remodeling the house and employ an odd little troop of helpers, huh?"

"Ya, I will need professional help, obviously. For one thing, I'm afraid of heights."

"Well, I know some women that do restoration. Lady carpenters, I have done some stuff with, but I can give you their names if you want. They will tell you the hard facts, and they get the work done."

"Great. Bob and Maria are helping clear the overgrowth, but we are slow. Maria loves the old gazebo and wants to make it a tent to sleep in. So, we are starting to get the prickers off and mowing the grass, Bob's good at that. He doesn't do it at home," she pointed at an octagonal structure partly cleared of the brambles.

"Wow, I can see the appeal of playing in that. And a little metal burn pit for a campfire, it looks like, right? You guys like to play with fire," Cake stepped carefully, ducking the hanging vines, and felt the vertical beams. "Seems steady."

Zsa-Zsa drank from the water dish set out as a lure for the Maine Coon. She licked up several kibbles left at the bottom of the bowl next to it. She lifted her head to sniff for the cat's scent that was lingering around the edges of the yard. The cat had been there recently. Scanning the long grass under the hedges for evidence, she thought she caught a shape in the shade on the other side of the fence. Nothing definite.

"There are several places motion lights could be put up, not too expensive or difficult to install. I could come and show you if you want." She drew a rough sketch of the ground plan and placed the lights in the best locations, marking them with a star and showed it to Oceanna.

"You are a talented artist too? This sketch is beautiful, complete and in proportion. I'm gonna frame it."

Cake laughed. "Let's try to get the hardware together and set a date to get them in soon."

"How about next week? I promised Maria and Bob we could have a cookout for Maria's birthday next Friday. We should have the gazebo cleared. She wants hot dogs cooked on a stick, with chili and onions. And Iced tea. You and Zsa-Zsa are welcome to join us if you want. Put the lights in. Get to know us better?" said Oceanna. "Margaritas, maybe?"

"Definitely." said Cake. "I'll bring the birthday cake, candles and ice cream."

"Chocolate!" Clapped Oceanna.

C H A P T E R   1 7 :

BUS STOP

Maria squeezed Bob's hand and tugged him around the sidewalk while they waited for the transport bus to take him to his job. Bob giggled and allowed her to drag him around in circles and tease him. She sang made-up songs in Spanish, and Bob tried to mouth her words and sing along.

"Mr. Bob, your Spanish is horrible. We must study how to pronounce. Right?"

"No!" said Bob and shook his head with a smile on his face.

"I am the teacher, and I say yes."

"No."

"You are not following the teacher's directions on purpose? That means you are defiant. Right?"

"No. Me, no."

"I'm gonna send you to the after-school detention if you don't study and do your homework!" She stood staunch with her hands on her narrow hips.

Bob shook his head and turned his back.

"This is wrong thinking! I have to arrest you now to go to detention, where the teachers are very mean. And you cannot eat at your desk!" She grabbed his belt from behind and tried to push him. He leaned back with his weight and did not budge. "And they will call your mother!"

Down the street two blocks away, Cake and Zsa-Zsa watched the antics from the cruiser with binoculars. She scanned the street for any people in their yards or out for a walk. She watched for cars with drivers that may circle back or sit watching suspiciously. She had photographed and listed the local cars and license plates and searched the files for any listed sex offenders that may be avoiding observation.

She and dog had given talks at the schools about Stranger Danger and presented how kids have been abducted in the past, asking for any information that may be relevant in these current cases. She had passed flyers and gone door to door, looked over the layout of alleys and overgrown parks. Nothing new. Now, she was observing Bob and Maria.

Patterns of behavior, she thought. Who enters the daily circle, everyday activities to stalk and grab a child? Is it an abrupt random attack? Most likely, it is planned very well in order to escape notice and hide so well. Someone is watching, waiting, maybe in plain sight. A person familiar with the daily routines of neighbors, noting who was vulnerable and who was protected.

How would she stalk for a victim, she wondered? How would she hide in plain sight and locate a victim? What tactics would she use to get away with an abduction? Bob and Maria were the most vulnerable people she had discovered. Now she would observe them to see them through the eyes of a stalker. She would learn by thinking like a killer. It was not a perfect strategy, but it was better than nothing.

In her rear-view mirror, she caught sight of the transport bus number 1313, rambling down the tree lined street about 5 blocks south of Bob's house. The driver waving now and then, stopping briefly to talk to children playing basketball on hoops positioned along the curbs.

"Signs of children," mumbled Cake to Zsa-Zsa, laying on her fleece blanket, drowsing. Kids come from blocks around to play on those hoops, she thought. No parents in sight. Scribbling her observation in her notebook, she wanted to appear preoccupied when the bus passed her.

It roared by and stopped respectfully at the cross street, then proceeded to pull over next to Bob and Maria, across the street from Bob's house, like every Monday, Wednesday, and Friday before, at 9:30 am. Then the door opened, and Bob got on. Cake could see most of Bob's details and the other passengers through the back window, specific shapes of heads in several seats as he sat down.

Maria appeared to be joking with the driver, laughing, and jumping up and down the entry stairs. Cake slipped the cruiser in gear and pulled up behind the bus, switching on the flashing lights and blowing her siren once, stopping at the rear bumper.

Maria covered her ears and hopped up and down. The driver jerked her head in alarm and looked hard in her rearview mirror as Cake stepped out of her car, put on her hat, and removed Zsa-Zsa, then approached the folding passenger door.

Greeting Zsa-Zsa with an open palm to her nose, Maria called out to the startled driver.

"That is my friend, Officer Cake, Lola!"

Cake hugged Maria and let her pet Zsa-Zsa while she stuck her head into the bus and addressed the flustered driver, Lola Kreem. Bob waved and grinned from his assigned seat. Cake took the name, number, and brief personal information from the driver when the dispatcher called out a situation needed a response. She gave her a business card and the flyer with the girl's descriptions and agreed to meet at her trailer home later, after the shift was over. Lola closed the door and quickly pulled away before Cake put dog into her car.

Maria's father's red, white, and blue dual-axle pickup pulled into their driveway down the street. She waved goodbye to Cake and galloped away home.

LOLA KREEM

Clicking off the TV, she downed her third beer and watched Cake pull up to her trailer with Zsa-Zsa in the passenger seat, driving a black Jeep in her civilian clothes. She admired the heavy bumper winch, wide toothy treaded tires and the extra row of amber lights on the roof.

"Flashy." Said Lola to herself. "Ready for any emergency. Heroic. Extra."

Her trailer was clean. No dishes in the sink or smudges on the tile. The bathroom had fresh toilet paper rolls and clean towels. She had done her laundry, no dirty rags. Her driver's uniforms had all been ironed and hung in the closet, and shoes wiped clean. The vacuum had been employed to suck up any hair or dust. Spotless.

She had even cleaned the grill and gotten a new tank of propane so the percolated coffee could be made outside, and the cooler was full of ice and beer. This could be a long conversation, and she wanted to be ready. She pulled the cellophane string to open a new pack of menthols, stuck one in between her dry lips and stepped out the door to greet her interrogators.

"Hey! You made it. My directions weren't too bad, heh," she stepped down the stairs and stuck her hand out for a shake.

Cake unsnapped dog's harness and brought her out with caution. She didn't want Zsa-Zsa to get too friendly, but she needed to make an olfactory record of Lola. She sniffed her extended hand before Cake shook it.

"Good evening, Ms. Kreem. I knew it was your spot from the bus parked next to your trailer. They let you bring it home every day?"

"Oh, yah. They save money on gas since I'm at the end of the line and can just go from home onto my route and back again. I make sure it's serviced, check oil and water, and the tires are full. All that daily. Come sit! Have coffee?" She looked up at Cake towering over her and asked. "You play soccer?"

"Nope. Track. Hurdles. They could never catch me," she grinned.

Lola nodded her head. "Damn! I'll bet. Well, have a seat at Lola's Grill. Coffee? Beer?"

Lighting the grill and putting the pot of coffee on. She pointed out one of the aluminum patio chairs set around a small table in the middle of a carpet of green Astroturf that was her patio, then cranked out a green and white striped canvas awning. Flipping a switch, she lit colored bulbs hanging from the fringe.

"Party time. Just coffee, thanks," said Cake taking a seat and stretching out her legs with dog laying very close and at ease.

Lola sat across and opened another beer. Tapping out another menthol, she offered one to Cake.

"Care for a smoke, ma'am?"

Cake felt ashamed as she accepted the offer immediately, pulling a cigarette from the pack. She remembered how hard it had been to quit the first time. Lola flicked the metal lighter lid open with a bright ring, thumbed the flint wheel, and brought a high flame to the smoke sticking out of her mouth, then leaned across the table to light Cake.

"Heh. Menthol is the best! I like the minty burn as it goes down," she grinned, showing gray teeth and a thick pink tongue.

Short, round and sturdy, she seemed surprisingly agile and moved fluidly around the patio. Cake pulled out her notebook and scribbled. Five-four? Busty, weight 180? Hair gray, eyes gray, bloodshot, bags. No rings or jewelry. No glasses.

"I'm here looking for any information you may have about the missing girls or any suspicious activity you may have noticed on your daily drive around the area of the missing girl's homes but . . . tell me first. Why are you living up against an auto junkyard?" said Cake. "When I pulled in, that was my first thought. The field is high with weeds and grass, the fence your trailer is up against is covered with berry bushes with thorns, the smell from the junk yard... is strong, what about this location is good?" she asked.

"Heh-heh. That is a good question, officer. That's easy, it's cheap!" Lola blew a cloud of smoke from her nose. "I don't pay more than a hundred dollars a month. I get free water and electricity hook up from the junkyard because I watch for burglars at night. I am the night watcher. Kids jump the back fence that's close to the 205 freeway, in the back twenty acres, pull up on a dirt bike or something, cut the chain links and steal a carburetor or something they can carry and poof! I'll show you around if you want."

Cake leaned back and scribbled. "Yes, that would be great. Wow, that's efficient. How do you do your rounds in the dark? The thieves could knock you out."

The coffee started to spit and bubble over the top of the pot, overheated by the flames. Lola hopped up and grabbed a hot mitt and a couple of large mugs. The smell of the burning coffee was pungent, but the smell of the junkyard was stronger. She mixed in the cream and sugar for both and plunked them on the table without asking how Cake took her's.

"I have a sidearm, officer. 45 caliber wheel gun. Registered for concealed carry. I have the papers. And I ride a little cart with headlights. I have fun, really. If I see anything going on, I call the cops," she sipped her coffee and lit another smoke.

The sunset was orange with wispy purple clouds and a sliver of moon on the rise. Crickets started to sing. Lola had no close neighbors. Her trailer was the only residence for blocks and was far enough back from the street that it was hardly noticeable. It might be thought abandoned at first glance, due to the overgrowth. The traffic noise from the street sounded a bit like water rushing over rocks, but the loaded semi-trucks shook the ground as they passed.

"How do you stand the smell? What is that? Oil and Gas? It's a strange mix."

"Oh, yah. And the noise of the tow motors can get to you. The sound of the crusher is scary. Now, that's a sound. They put the hole car in the hopper, and these giant hydraulic jaws come around the car and fold and squeeze it into a block that weighs about a ton. The metal creaks and squeaks, and the glass shatters . . . that's the quiet part! Heh, the engine it uses is a dilly. Really loud and smoky. Black oil smoke out of the exhaust pipe. Yikes. When they get a full load crushed, a semi comes, and they load the blocks on the trailer, three high and off they go, across the sea!" she looked up from her coffee into Cake's eyes. "You can't hear yourself scream over that mess."

"I see," she said as she scribbled. "The crusher. Deafening."

There was a gleam in Lola's eyes. She smiled as she spoke, pulled hard on her cigarette, and seemed amused.

"I'll take a beer," said Cake.

"Oh great! Me too. It was getting a bit stuffy out here. Heh," she pulled two from under the ice, popped the lids and slid one bottle across the table. "Here's to ya," said Lola before chugging down half the bottle.

A large dial thermometer hanging next to the front door read 91 degrees. The sliver moon was bright as the sky darkened. A few stars twinkled.

"So, what is up with Bob and the sanitarium? Dolly Smack said it was called the 'asylum for the feeble-minded' Fill me in. Dolly said you helped there. Do you know Bob? And can I get a bowl of water for Zsa-Zsa?"

Lola dumped the bowl of sugar packets out on the table and filled the bowl with ice and some of the water from the ice that had melted and slid it over to dog, who was panting and lapped it up with sloppy noises. A slight breeze came up, cooling the perspiration on Cake's brow. Without the direct sun, the temperature dropped ten degrees.

Lola looked at the ground in thought.

"Well, the sign on the gate tells ya what you need to know. The place was a hell hole. That's the way to describe it. The kids were brought in, months old maybe, several years old with some kind of deformity, cleft pallet or seizures, behavior issues or low I.Q. or what not . . . and they never left," her expression went dark. She drank the beer that was left and pulled another from the cooler, popped the lid and drank half of it.

"What do you mean? The kids never left," Cake asked and pointed at the pack of smokes, asking for another. Lola slid the pack over to her and lit it once she had it in her lips.

"It was a life sentence, officer! If you were sick or strange, if you made the doctors and parents uncomfortable, you got dropped off at the door, and that was it. There was no cure for birth defects or . . . whatever, so, the doctors in those days just got rid of them. They told the mothers it was hopeless and not to come back."

"When did Bob go in?"

"Oh, when he was a little guy, about five years old. Grew like a weed. They say he burned down the house! With his father in it! A police sergeant! They say it was because he was abusive. Beat the mom and drank. Oh, yeh! That was a big story the nurses told."

"Tell me some details about this. Did you think he was dangerous? Sexual?"

Cake dipped the water bowl into the ice water at the bottom of the cooler again and gave it to Zsa-Zsa with a favorite dog biscuit from her pocket. She wagged her tail and crunched it with her long white fangs immediately. Cake resumed scribbling.

"Well, Dolly Smack was a very young strip dancer, a good one, so they say, and Bob's dad was an older cop, drank heavy and played around. I guess they got married. I don't think Bob Sr. enjoyed the fact that his son was a mental cripple. That's the word. Dad couldn't love him. He beat the wife for her mistake, I guess, and Bob too. A lot of men do that. It's macho."

"How did they know Bob burned the house, I wonder? He doesn't talk," said Cake.

"I don't know that. It might still be in a file somewhere with your guys. Dad was a cop, so there must be something."

"If the asylum was a life sentence, how did Bob get out?" Cake asked, looking at the sunset in its last colors, wondering what Bob's life must have been like.

Lola tapped out another smoke and grabbed another beer. Her eyes looked misty, and her muscles loosened.

"He lucked out. One of the nurses died right at the nurse's station. A friend of mine named Ambrosia. Nurse Ambrosia. Pills she took from the patients, downed with gin. Overdosed and lay her head on the desk, and bam. Heart attack. The place was run like that. It started an investigation, and bingo, the whole place was a mess. They found cremated patient ashes in unmarked urns, children tied to their cribs, filthy diapers. Patients tied to wheelchairs all day. Ya, lots of neglect. It was a nightmare."

"Did you see the abuse? Why stay?"

"I transported most of the time. I admit I just wanted a job, and I thought if the Doctors thought it was . . . ok?"

"Didn't the families visiting see things?" asked Cake.

"I tell you, they told mothers not to visit! Out of sight, out of mind? Heh, that was Doc's advice! So, finally, the families sued the crap out of the place and won. No more government funding? Goodbye, asylum."

"Ya, I get it. But how old was Bob when he got out?" She stopped scribbling and looked up.

"About fifteen. He lucked out, went back to his mom. They got some settlement money to live on. I got a job transporting the guys from group homes to workshops and day programs that the administrators started. Totally different life with rights," she opened another beer and offered it to Cake. "Heh, so what about the missing girls?"

"Have you seen the girls in the poster I gave you?"

"No." Lola burped.

"You haven't seen kids walking to school? You are driving at those times, aren't you?" The sunset turned cobalt blue, and the sliver moon shone. The fringe lights cast colorfully on the table.

"No, there are lots of kids walking at that time." She smiled. "Pretty sunset."

The conversation paused. They leaned their heads back and looked at the evening stars in silence. A breeze blew over the high weeds, bending them in waves. Cake sketched the layout of the trailer's location as it butted up against the junk yard's overgrown chain link fence, the position of the gravel driveway, the location of the bus parking spot, the tool shed just behind the trailer, approximate distances between the street to the trailer and the acer of weeds to the next neighbor and the 205 freeway exit and entry ramp on the other side of the junkyard.

"It's late." said Cake. "I appreciate your time. . . . keep your eyes open for suspicious activity. I want to continue our conversation another day, later."

"Perfect, Heh, heh, next time, bring a pizza!" laughed Lola.

CHAPTER 19:
HELP AT THE HAUNTED HOUSE

Hot and breezy, sweet fragrances lifting off the lilacs and wide-open roses as Maria's ninth birthday arrived. Blackberries ripe and fat hung heavily in bunches along Oceanna's fence. Days of trimming and pruning, mowing, and sweeping brought the backyard closer to better but far from finished. After Bob mowed and edged most of the driveway and bristle brushed the flagstone paths from moss and weeds so they glistened in the sun, showing white and gray along the foundation, Oceanna handed him a crisp Twenty-dollar bill and one for Maria.

Maria picked bowls full of berries and wanted to make a pie. Her fingers were stained red from the juice, her face and lips, smeared with the same. She imagined Dream, steaming in the sun, curled up on the freshly mowed lawn, flicking her long black tail and munching grass. Drowsy, peaceful, and safe.

The gazebo had been freed from thorns, mounds of dry fall leaves swept away, and spiders sent sprinting up their webs. Maria dusted and washed the bench seating around the sides, hoping to create a bunk bed for overnight sleepovers.

Oceanna strung red Chinese party lanterns across the yard and piled charcoal and wood into the metal fire pit. Sparks twinkled, and flames fluttered as Maria poked them with a stick. Coolers chilled with ice, root beer, hot dogs, relish, mustard, hot sauce and onions. Homemade chili bubbled in the cast iron pot cooking on the grate.

Cake arrived looking unfamiliar in jeans and a sleeveless tee shirt, carrying a homemade devil's food cake, with nine candles, ice cream and gift boxes under her arms. Zsa-Zsa wore a red, white, and blue bandana around her neck with a birthday card taped to it. She wagged her tail as Maria hugged her neck. Maria insisted the candles be lit immediately because she had a perfect wish and wanted it to get going right away. She jumped for joy and cried while blowing out the flames, triggering Oceanna to weep. They sang the birthday song and hugged each other.

Tearing open the boxes, Maria marveled at the real walkie-talkies and polished brass Junior Officer badge, Cake had delivered. Cake showed them how to wear the holsters when on guard, how to turn them on and off, dial in a frequency to match their partners, signal S-O-S on the Morris-Code button, and talk like a detective. Cake roamed out on the sidewalk in front of the house with Zsa-Zsa at her heels while Maria and Bob walked up and down the street, hopping in and out of driveways, seeing how far they could go before the connection was cut out.

Maria and Dream galloped ahead, leaving Bob to walk back alone. Cake gave a set to Oceanna for rapid direct communication with her in case of trouble and practiced signaling with her from the tower. Oceanna could see the activity of the others on the street clearly and gave away their locations during a game of hide and seek.

At dinner, Bob and Maria toasted hot dogs on extended telescopic forks. After two hot dogs with chili and onions for Maria, and four dogs with chili, relish, and cheese for Bob, two overcooked ones for Zsa-Zsa, two bowls of chili for Oceanna and two chili cheese dogs for Cake. Maria and Bob rolled onto freshly padded recliners held their bellies, and dozed, saving the cake for after a nap.

As the sun set behind the West Hills, the sky went bluer. Shadows got longer. Patrol dogs and fantasy horses snored on the grass, giving a few moments for adults to talk and Oceanna's bartender skills to be employed, mixing margaritas to be sucked on.

"Good Margarita, very limey!" said Cake, leaning back in her chair, chewing the salt off the wide rim of a glass decorated with tiny glass cactus plants all around the stem.

"Margaritas and vodka Martinis are my specialties." said Oceanna clinking her glass on Cake's.

"Are you a Mixologist then?"

"Oh, yah! I have tended bars for years up and down the coast. And I'm usually the one chosen to be the mixer at parties, as well as the designated driver."

"You take care of others a lot. Do you get tired of it? I see you healing people and situations, intervening in helpful ways, right?" said Cake.

"Well, I don't know about that. Rough attempts to help, maybe," she blushed.

"It's a beautiful trait. You take care of Vivian and her enticing runaway ambition. You take care of Maria, a complete stranger, even after she scared you that first day, and Bob, with his unusual ways. Teaching them how to do things around here, letting them play. They earn a little money and . . . me and Zsa-Zsa today, inviting us into your little gang of misfits? You're a nice lady, Anna," raising her glass, she extended her long arm across the table to toast her.

"Thank you, Cake. Now, I don't feel so alone," Oceanna smiled weakly.

C H A P T E R   2 0 :

LIGHTNING STRIKES

"I have to pack all this stuff up onto the display cards for quick set up, Anna. I have to take as much as I can because I think it's going to be a big big day for CozmetixX and Vivian Lash's Toys For Joys! I can feel it! I'm going to pack the toys in these crates with wheels. They get heavy, and I can't move them in and out of the van. I'm not a monster like you!" she said, looking over her shoulder at Oceanna lifting the tubs of toys and costumes onto a dolly. She brushed the black velvet display shelves, gingerly and slid them into the slots in the crates for safe transport.

"Right," replied Oceanna.

"The crowds are huge down at Waterfront on any Saturday, but on the fourth of July? It gets scary! It's a sea of people!"

"Shoulder to shoulder. It's the all-day live music and fireworks that brings 'um. Sunny Moon and the Satellites will be on just before the fireworks. Perfect," said Oceanna.

Lifting a bucket of hot soapy water onto the window seats, she examined the convex windowpanes and wooden frames of the tower, wondering how she would wash the outside without climbing a forty-foot ladder. Her stomach fluttered at the simple thought of climbing a ladder to change the light bulbs in the living room's eight-foot-high fixtures. She felt dizzy looking out over the landscape of rooves and treetops, beyond the bridges spanning the Willamette River into downtown.

"Storm's coming. Black clouds over the hills," said Oceanna. Thunder rolled and pounded in the distance. "It's coming. Lightening flashing around the city."

A summer storm, crackled in jagged lightning spears, whipping through the black clouds, lashing at the towers through the mist. Lights popped on and off in the expensive houses perched on the cliffs. Webs of light flashed among the clouds, and the wind rushed. Gusts rattled the glass and twisted trees. Bats, shaken awake, jostled, peeped, squeezing tightly together in their narrow hide-e- holes in the eves. Oceanna watched them hug their wings over their heads and hang on.

Overlooking the neighborhood, she watched Maria hopping around her yard, playing horse ranch around the pull-behind camper and her father's pride and joy Ford, in front of the house. Ten houses down the street, Oceanna could see Bob rocking on his porch swing, blissfully off in a world of his own. A light came on in Dolly's upstairs bedroom window. She came to the window, looked out for a moment, her long gray hair fluttering around her head, pulled the curtains in and shut it, as the black clouds rolled over them, shadowing the streets into dusk.

Suddenly, the rain blasted down in a wall of water. Maria squealed and ran into the house. Through the large living room window, Oceanna watched Ralfie flip on the porch light and help Maria light a fire in the fireplace. Thunder collided with the earth and shook it.

"This is a wonderful surveillance spot; Officer Cake is right. You can see everything," mumbled Oceanna.

"Officer Cake comes around for visits? How often does she do that?" she said, looking over her shoulder. "You are messing around with her while I am slaving to make a buck?" Viv unfolded leather bondage garments from the display box, and stretched a black leather muzzle around her face in a taunt. "Slaving? Get it? Look, Ma'am."

"Ok. I get it, Viv," she said, shaking her head.

"These are some of my newer items, dear. We haven't tried them, yet. Quit staring out at the neighbors, and we can see how these fit." she purred.

"Ok, dear. As long as you are the one wearing it," said Oceanna jumping down from the window seat. "You're the noisy one! Let's try it on you first."

Viv dodged Oceanna, putting the round table between them, singing, "Catch me if you can."

Oceanna snatched the leather straps in a quick leap and pulled them both down to the floor, wrestling to get the upper hand.

They stopped playing abruptly. Air pressure seemed to be changing, building up around them. Their ears felt like they were underwater. Their skin tingled, and static snapped through the air. As they stared at each other, Vivian's eyes grew wide. Her long black hair began to lift upward and outward from her head, standing on end, all around, like the fluff of a dandelion. Oceanna's short mop stuck out from her tingling scalp, like a cartoon character in surprise. They laughed nervously. Oceanna reached out to feel Vivian's wild mane when the room exploded.

The tower flashed in an enormous white-hot spark. Millions of volts shattered the atmosphere. The air became power. Flesh became hot, charged through every cell. For an instant, bodies became lanterns. The lightning flattened them to the floor, unconscious and smoldering. Shelves of glass jars holding herbs and healing potions blew up, scattering the ingredients, dusting the room with fragrance. Wooden beams of the tower roof shivered and smoked. Bats fell from their nests into the room, stunned, onto the rugs and bodies below.

Oceanna woke slowly, tingling, and paralyzed. Bats, shocked and confused, rained down from the roof and crawled over her. She breathed in deeply, feeling sharp pain when her ribs expanded. Her body felt too heavy to lift at first. She wiggled her fingers to see if she had any. Little by little, she found movement returning to her fingers, then hands, up to her elbows. She wiggled her toes and bent her knees, struggling to sit up and check Vivian for life signs. She lay smoldering, inches away, still out.

Minutes passed before Oceanna was convinced, she was still whole, and Vivian opened her eyes. Vision was blurry but returning. Hearing was dulled but became more acute with each passing minute. They spoke in whispers because their throats felt burnt and sore.

Rolling over onto their backs, orienting, they lay still, taking in air and letting their eyes focus on the movement of strange lights around them. Bats stirred, wobble-crawling up the walls of the tower, clumsily feeling for toe holds, wanting desperately to return to their tight cubbies, but they were changed. Their black bodies glowed with a luminous lavender haze, and their eyes popped gold.

Reasoning that her eyes were tricking her, Oceanna blinked and did not remark about her perceived hallucinations to Vivian.

"There are purple bats crawling around us, Anna. That's unusual, let's agree?" Viv said, looking around the room for confirmation that it was real.

As they lay on their backs staring at the roof, it became clear that the lavender light was glowing from the elaborate design of the tower beams. The lavender mist hung around them, filled with gold sparks floating down like snowflakes, twinkling softly, then evaporating.

"Look at that. I never noticed the design before," said Oceanna.

"The beams are shining in a star?" Viv sighed.

"It's a pentagram like the inlay of the card table. It's a message," head spinning and body aching and stiff, Oceanna got to her knees and took Viv's hands, yanking her up to a sitting position, leaning her back against the table leg. Using the table, she pulled herself up to stand.

The tabletop was singed. The rose scented candles had melted and drooped. The box that held the deck of Tarot cards had flown open, spitting the cards out over the room. One bat floundered on the table, unable to find it's way. Oceanna picked it up cautiously. It struggled in her palm and blinked at her through fresh gold eyes. She set it on a shelf where the jars had been, giving it time to find a path back up. It peeped faintly and licked it's nose with a flickering red tongue in gratitude. Lavender goo stuck to her fingers. She tasted it. Hot mint.

She noticed a book, thick, leather bound, fizzing, spitting gold sparks like a fire work sparkler from the top shelf of the bookcase, with silver calligraphic lettering that shone like a mirror. Feeling drawn, she clambered slowly up a short ladder, clinging to the rail, and pulled it down, luminescence flowed like honey over the bindings. It was dry to the touch as it rolled from the book onto Oceanna's hands and forearms, fading before it hit the floor.

Oceanna read the title to Viv.

"Book Of Sisters," Read Oceanna, while Vivian squinted at the bats.

C H A P T E R   2 1 :

BLACKOUT

Lightning struck the power transfer stations, knocking out the electricity to thousands of homes across the southeast. Fires caused by the oil in the transformer cases overheated and burned hot, giving firefighters few options but to let the oil burn out rather than electrocuting the neighborhoods by forcing water on them; the rain was bad enough.

The street gutters raged with fast-flowing runoff. Leaves washed into drains, plugging the grates. Water pooled in the intersections and streets twelve inches deep. Cars stalled mid-way, trying to get past them. Tow trucks worked to drag them out with winches. Streets were dark and chaotic; people at bus stops cowered under umbrellas if they could, strangers sharing out of pity. Rain fell in buckets.

Cake and Zsa-Zsa were on their way home from another long day when the transformers blew. They maneuvered through side streets, trying not to become the next emergency. The storm-battered tree limbs, snapping them off, dropping them into the narrow streets below. Cake pulled several huge limbs to the side, freeing pathways for drivers that were hoping to get home. Thunder rattled the Jeep; dog laid her head down on the stick shift and put her ears back. Cake pet her head to reassure her. The windshield fogged up, and a leak drizzled in through a seam in the canvas roof. She cranked the defroster high. The Jeep's lift kit she had installed was working to give them clearance through deep water as they crawled their way to their favorite street.

Electricity was out on both sides of the street, but the flooding was not too deep. Maria's front window glowed yellow from the fire in their fireplace. She couldn't see details through the fogged window, but silhouettes moved around in a relaxed manner, so they were probably not in need of help. Ralfie's truck was a high four-wheel drive, so they could get out if they had to.

Driving by Oceanna's place, she saw a strange lavender atmosphere in the tower windows with the rest of the lights out. Vivian's CozmetixX van was in the driveway, so she imagined they were taking care of each other and were safe. Cake stopped and looked up at the house. She rolled the details of their relationship over in her mind. Oceanna, feeling alone and insecure. Vivian is dominant and ambitious.

"Love and money, Zsa-Zsa. The two things we want most that will drive you to despair trying to get. And if you do, troubles. Love is a sugar-coated tragedy waiting to happen." she said quietly to dog, petting her long ears while she thought. "It's the longing that kills me. That is painful. You fall in love and then spend your time longing for them. Well, good luck, ladies," putting the rig in first, they rolled down to Bob and Dolly's place.

The Cake got out, and the rain pounded in. She grabbed a waterproof flashlight and flipped it onto the wide beam. She opened dog's passenger door, unsnapped her safety harness, and commanded heel. She jumped out and stayed by her partner's side, understanding they were working now. She followed Cake's long strides through the gate and up the stairs onto the covered porch; they were already soaked. Cake pounded firmly on the door.

"Bob and Dolly Smack! It's Officer Emerald Cake and Zsa-Zsa checking on safety. Are you alright? Your lights are out, and I'm worried.

Please respond." she banged several times more. She tried to shine the light through the opaque glass in the door but couldn't see movement. She knocked again, louder, considering what to do next. The rain clattered on the porch roof, potentially covering any cries for help.

Then, she heard thumping, maybe heavy footfalls on a wooden stair, and a faint holler from a woman. Her heart jumped. She yelled she was coming in, backed up several feet and lifted her knee, aimed her foot, and prepared to kick the door in, when movement could be seen on the other side of the glass, and the deadbolt turned. Bob pulled open the door, weeping and flustered.

"Ma, fall! Over there!" He began to cry and wring his hands.

"Ok, Bob! We are here to help. Show us!" She gave him a short hug and gave him the flashlight to show the way. Dog remained at her partner's side, ready and panting. Bob trotted up the staircase to the second floor, down a hall and across a generous master bedroom, and into a large bathroom where Dolly lay crumpled and naked.

"Bob, hold the light on your mother. Dolly, It's Officer Cake to help you. Are you alright? Anything broken, as far as you can tell?"

She knelt down and looked into her eyes to see if Dolly's pupils were even. No blood or vomit. No pills or bottles of alcohol. She palpated her legs and arms for a break.

Her slender body almost glowed in the dark; she was so pale. Her long wet hair lay in tangles around her neck and face. Cake lifted the hair away from her cheeks to check for cuts. Her face was smooth; her lips were gray. Cake pulled a towel over her breasts.

Dolly reached up and took Cake's hand, pulled her closer, and held it tightly to her chest. Her heart was racing. Her deep breathing blew across Cake's cheek. Her breath smelled like mint. They lingered for a moment, looking at each other. Bob kept crying and asking if Dolly was alright.

"I think I'm ok, Bobby; I just fell, baby. You saved mother. Just shaken and embarrassed," she smiled at Cake's serious expression. "Maybe bruised?"

The towel rack was broken, dragged off the wall, and the shower curtain was torn down, implying she had slipped and tried to hang on to something to stabilize herself, leading to a collapse on the floor. Luckily, there was a rug that softened the fall.

"Should I call an ambulance?" said Cake.

"Oh, no! No! I slipped in the tub when the lights went out," said Dolly.

"Are you able to stand?" asked Cake. Zsa-Zsa came up and licked her partner's arm for reassurance.

"Good Girl, Zsa-Zsa, sit. She followed instructions and squeezed into a sitting position between herself and the cabinets.

"Can you stand, Dolly? It's getting crowded in here."

"Can you lift me to the bed? I can sit up and try my legs from there," she smiled and put her arms around Cake's neck.

Sliding her arms around Dolly's hips carefully, she lifted her wet body from the floor with Zsa-Zsa and Bob close behind. Dolly clung to her neck with her nose close to Cake's ear. She lifted Dolly with ease, her body feeling like a feather in her arms. Bob held the light on the king-sized bed, glistening in the flashlight's shine, tangled black satin sheets. The wallpaper reflected silver.

Cake lifted Dolly gingerly, in case of fracture, carried her to the bedside, and slowly set her down. Her hands slipped across the space between her buttocks and her thin thighs. Her fingers traced her body's curves unavoidably. Cake felt a stir inside.

Holding Dolly excited her. She felt ashamed. She had reservations about Dolly's innocence and needed to be able to think clearly about her influence in several matters, including the missing girls. Becoming attracted to the suspect was not allowed and may be dangerous. She fought the thrill of feeling Dolly's wet body against her chest, her legs draped over her arms, the smell and feel of her body so close.

"Thank you, Emerald. I owe you one," said Dolly as she leaned into Cake's embrace, sliding her cheek across Cake's lips. Bob stood behind, still holding the flashlight.

"Bobby, light the candles, darling. But first, bring me a robe, please, honey. From the closet, darling Bobby, please help Mother," he stood frozen. "It's ok; you can use the matches this time, honey."

Bob sorted through several nightgowns in the long walk-in closet filled with flashy clothing, holding up one hanger after the other. Finally, finding the one she wanted and brought it to her, still sitting exposed on the bed.

"Will you join me for one of Bob's super Martinis, Emerald? This must have been a hard night for you. We would love to spend more time with you, Bob, and I?" She smiled softly, speaking in a near whisper. "I spend so much time alone. I'm thirsty for good company."

Bob held up a sheer silk nightgown. Dolly waved her hand, signaling him to bring it over.

Cake smiled nervously, hiding her desire. Zsa-Zsa wagged her wet tail. Bob opened the gown and held it up for Dolly to dawn. The gossamer slid over her body. She took hold of Cake's arm for help going down the stairs. How could she refuse? Her stomach rolled over. Getting involved with a suspect would definitely complicate her investigation. She felt both sexy and sick.

DOLLY AND CAKE TALK HISTORY

Bob gathered candles and oil lamps, striking red-headed matches to their wicks, adjusting the flames low to lessen the smoke as they burned. He opened the gas fireplace and lit the realistic ceramic logs that heated the room.

Cake and Dolly descended the stairs together. Dolly seemed to float over the floor. The Cake took off her wet sweatshirt, laid it over the arm of the couch, leaving her in a thin tank top, and directed Zsa-Zsa to sit. She held Dolly's hand to lower her onto her cushions.

"The room is so beautiful with all the candles, Bobby. You are such a good son. Perfect baby. Thank you," she blew a kiss at him, making him giggle.

"I know, Ma."

"Is everyone alright?" said Cake standing in the middle of the room, making sure the tragedy had been averted. Bob nodded. Dolly pulled her feet up under her and patted the cushion next to her.

Zsa-Zsa licked her lips and panted. She had been thinking of dinner, going home to her own bed, and calling it a night. Now, she could only hope that Bob would bring her a piece of cheese or a hotdog like he had at Maria's Birthday party. She lay down and watched.

"Come and sit next to me, Emerald. Let me show you, my portfolio. I promised you I would show you how it used to be. And let's have some refreshments after all this! Bob? Please bring in the cart and mix up some special Martinis, darling. Ok, Officer?"

Cake hesitated, still standing, feeling uncertain about the trajectory of the evening. Looking at Dolly in the dim light, she could have been twenty years younger, flirtatious, and playful. The shine of her gown was iridescent. Her allure was dizzying. She sat slowly, leaving some polite space between them, like she was lowering herself into a ridiculously hot Jacuzzi, slowly getting used to the heat on the way down.

Bob, happy to please, trotted into the kitchen and clanked glass onto the cart. Zsa-Zsa watched him through the kitchen door.

"And bring some water and a treat for Zsa-Zsa; she helped save Mother too," she blew a kiss to dog. "You seem very strong; what is your sport? What did you do with those long legs of yours? Tennis?"

"Marathons. I have stamina," she smiled, folding her knees between the glass coffee table and the couch.

"Well . . . my money's on you, darling," grinned Dolly.

Bob wheeled the chrome bar cart into the living room. First, giving attention to Zsa-Zsa's water bowl with a side of hot dogs. Starting on the drinks, he set up two stemmed, wide-lipped glasses, skewered two queen-sized green olives with red centers, and dropped them into the glasses. Then, with panache, he dashed chilled vodka with a splash of olive brine into the glasses, finally drizzling in strange dark vermouth carefully. It spiraled and shone with a luminous lavender light in a thin ribbon throughout the drink. Handing one to Mother, she winked. Cake eyed the lavender threading through the vodka.

"Here's to you and your partner; you were right on time to save me." Dolly leaned over and clinked Cake's glass.

"Almost like it was planned," said Cake.

"Well, you are an officer, always suspicious. Looking for clues?" She drank the Martini dry and held her glass out to Bob for a refill. Cake sipped hers for taste.

"Are you afraid of me, Emerald?"

"Well . . . yes. You are pretty hard to resist," she drank her cocktail in small sips. Feeling the vodka absorbed in her throat and the unusual flavor of the lavender on her tongue.

"Resist? Why resist?" She slid her hips an inch closer to Cake until she was up against her thigh. "I don't bite. Right away."

Cake saw a flash in Dolly's gray eyes. Feeling herself being drawn in, she took another sip. The usual anxiety she felt in romantic situations did not disturb her this time. A calm wave massaged her better judgment. She felt foggy, slow, and easy, as though she was being dipped in romantic honey.

Bob was ready with another set of drinks, filled Dolly's glass, then Cake's. Popping a root beer, he turned on a small radio, settled into his recliner next to the fireplace, closed his eyes, and rocked.

Dolly dragged the fat portfolio from the coffee table onto her lap and flopped the cover open onto Cake's leg next to her.

"Look, this is me at seventeen. I got into a dance job by pretending I was eighteen. The guy didn't care, and as you can see . . . I could pass. I made my own costumes."

"You had a professional look. Good headshots, the lighting is great," Cake smiled.

"What about the costumes?"

"The costumes look . . . very small," said Cake. Dolly looked disappointed. "And you look incredible in them."

"Thank you," said Dolly as she flipped the page.

"When did you meet Bob's father? You must have been pretty young?"

"Yes. I was dancing for about a year. Various clubs. And Bob Senior would come in for lunch and drinks while on duty. He was handsome and strong. He was proud in his uniform and tipped well. Very polite and very intense. I was attracted to him, but I was careful; he was a cop and might be trouble. He was about twice my age, with graying hair, but I liked that. Mature and romantic. Seemed strong and safe. That's him in his dress blues," she pointed to an eight by ten of Bob Smack Sr., ruggedly handsome, severe and square-jawed, brass polished and trimmed.

"You fell for him fast?"

"Yeah, at first, I tried to avoid him, but the attraction was too strong. He came in one night with long stem roses and got on one knee. I was nineteen and had nothing to lose. The whole thing was in front of everyone while I was on stage. It was shocking and romantic, and I gave in. We got married in Las Vegas real fast. It was fine at first, but his jealousy got to be too much after a while, so I quit dancing, got pregnant soon after. Bobby was born one year after we were married."

"Sounds very deep. What happened?" She reached down to pet the dog while she snored.

"Alcohol and his need to own me. He started to drink and stay out as I got bigger with Bobby. Sex was uncomfortable, and he looked at other dancers. He was a smooth talker. A lady's man. I fell for him, so why wouldn't they?"

She opened a bottle of pills from the group of prescriptions collected on the side table and took two, downing them with her drink. Reaching across the table, she lifted the vodka, chilling in a bucket of ice, and poured it into her glass. She lit a cigarette for herself and one for Cake and put it between her lips.

"I imagine you fought over this," said Cake as she inhaled, surprised at not feeling guilty.

"Horribly. Violently. He started to beat me for complaining and got rough with the sex right up to the birth. That may be what happened to Bobby. I don't know. He was enraged."

"Rape?"

"I called it that. Often. Little Bobby would hide in Mother's closet with his toys and cry. His dad beat him for that. Called him all the names. Fag and retard. Bob Senior was not proud of a son that could not talk and played with dolls. He made us stay in the house. So, he was mad at both of us, and it all went to hell. Funny how he was so macho and fragile at the same time. Typical," she leaned her shoulder sideways, pressing onto Cake.

"I guess the cops covered for him."

"Brothers in arms. It's a double-edged sword. They ignored his drinking and wife beating but took care of us after he died."

"So, what actually happened to him?" asked Cake in a whisper, feeling floaty and euphoric, enjoying the feel of Dolly's weight.

"He died when the house burned down around him, drunk in bed," she spat out quickly and sighed, then looked at Cake. For a moment, they were still.

"Tell me," said Cake.

"I think he smoked in bed and passed out. It could have been that . . . or. They blamed Bobby because some neighbors had seen him playing with matches in the backyard, and he had set some weeds on fire one time. Nothing big. They never proved it was Bob. He was only five years old. But they figured it was Bobby and he was strange; I tried to defend him, but they determined he was a dangerous kid, and I was in shock and confused. I had just lost my husband and my home, and I really didn't know. The psychiatrists pressured me to give him up. I agreed to commit him. I will never forgive myself," she began to cry.

Cake put her arm around her. Pulled her closer.

"Do you think Bobby set the fire? After all the years?"

"I don't know. They took him to that horrible mental hospital down south. The psychiatrists said it would tear me apart to go see him. They told all of us mothers that junk. The judge said it would be heartbreaking, and he would never get better and all that. I thought I could get him out after a few months or something. I had no idea it was for good. That or prison? I thought about killing myself a million times; the hope of getting him out kept me going."

"What happened after they took him? What did you do?" asked Cake as Dolly leaned into her shoulder and held her hand.

"I drank, did drugs, felt lousy, got prescriptions for depression and whatever. Crap that was the worst. The fire insurance rebuilt the house, as you see it now. The policeman's pensions saved me. I just lowered my head and became a virtual hermit. I hate that I didn't get him out. You see how Bobby turned out to spite his lousy childhood. A real gentleman, thank you."

Sitting and rocking to his own beat. Bob drifted off. Relaxed by the fire.

"Thank God I had gotten to know some of the neighbors like Oceanna's grandmother living in the tower," she flipped to a picture of Bob as a child swinging with a little girl that looked like Oceanna and her grandmother Blanch, pushing her swing.

"When did Bob get out?" asked Cake, wondering if Dolly's story would match Lola's, and tucked Dolly's head under her chin. She untied her bandana from her neck and gave it up for drying tears.

"He was a grown man, tall at fifteen. When the place finally got shut down, they got caught for neglecting the kids. They found all kinds of abuse going on. Who knows what really happened?"

Dolly reached over and stroked Cake's chest. She could feel her heartbeat and smell her fresh fragrance.

"God knows what they did to Bobby and what the whole array of horrors was. Bobby never said anything. The upside is that all of us family members got settlement money, and Bob gets a monthly sum for the rest of his life. The weird thing is it was like he never left. We just march to a similar drum. I take care of him, and he takes care of me, as you can see."

Cake felt the thrill of being wanted and thought she should be resisting, but the urge was too strong; she panted and didn't move.

Dolly shifted slowly onto her knees, pulled up her gown, straddled Cake's lap, pulled her hand under her, and sat on her long fingers. Dolly's smooth wet lips fit into her palm like a glove. She rolled over her fingers, feeling open, and Cake's fingers enter. She pressed and undulated gracefully and in no rush. Pulling Cake's head back, she kissed her deeply, sucking her tongue into her mouth, feeling Cake inside herself, deeply, as much as she could. The Cake came with a shudder and a gasp. Dolly climaxed with a spray of her juices. They were soaked.

A siren howled faintly from a distance and got louder as the rescue vehicle tracked to another emergency. It seemed to be wandering through the dark side streets. Flashing red lights fluttered faintly across Dolly's curtains. Cake's head cleared slightly. Zsa-Zsa stood and went to the front door, pressing her nose to the latch.

This was not supposed to happen, she thought to herself. She already regretted it. She shifted Dolly off of her lap. Dolly clung to her and kissed her, trying to hold her close. Cake hugged her, laid her on the couch pillows, and stood.

"This was not supposed to happen," Cake whispered apologetically and smiled.

"Oh yes, it was, Officer. Don't be sorry for a thing. You're beautiful; now, duty calls, get going. I'm more than fine," She scanned Cake self-indulgently, watching her broad shoulders and bronze arms disappear as she slipped into her sweatshirt.

"Will you pour me another drink, Emerald?" Dolly opened a pill bottle and took two more onto her tongue and held up her glass.

"Please be careful with that, Dolly," said Cake as she pulled the vodka from the ice and poured another, stabbed an olive, and dropped it in. She lifted the lavender liquid up to her eye and watched it bubble and swirl. Zsa-Zsa barked at the door and shook her head.

"What is this purple stuff?"

"Very special stuff. Secret," she smiled. "You better go."

The ambulance rolled past the house, red and white emergency lights flashing. The siren cut off. Cake moved to the door, pulled it open, and looked back at Dolly, eyeing her back.

"See you later. Come again," she laughed.

Zsa-Zsa growled at the flashing lights, trotted out of the door, down the stairs to her Jeep, wagged her tail and whined to get in. The rain had stopped, but the streets were still flooded and dark. Still misty from the magic martinis, Cake pulled away from the curb, slowly splashing through glistening dark pools down the street. Dog panted, looking alert from the passenger seat. Cake scratched dog's back.

"Thanks, girl. I owe you for getting me out," she sighed. "I'm getting us some cheeseburgers."

C H A P T E R 2 3 :

BOOK OF SISTERS

Bob hardly needed the ladder to reach the chandelier bulbs and wall fixtures. Oceanna got vertigo at the lowest rungs, so it was worth twenty dollars to have Bob help her. The old ornate fixtures looked best with fake flame-style bulbs, and they offered a soft, soothing yellow light. She had tried several brands, some that flickered, casting moving shadows around the room that irritated her, so she stuck with the simple yellow flames.

The nightmare of removing the old wallpaper was over. Cake helped greatly by showing Oceanna how to use a steamer and lent days of help prepping the lath and plaster walls for a smooth paint application.

Maria wanted to paint the walls and ceilings and practiced walking on the carpenter's twelve-inch stilts around the living room. She had assembled the roller and telescopic pole, practicing reaching the high spots with a clean roller, promising to be ready to follow Oceanna after she painted around the corners and windowsills. The wooden window frames had been masked off, and all the fixtures had been removed; furniture had been moved into the middle of the room and covered with canvas sheets. Soon the fun part of putting on color could begin.

There came a banging at the door.

"I'll get it!" yelled Maria staggering to the door on her stilts. She peeked through the door's peephole. "It's Officer Cake and Zsa-Zsa! Come in. It's not locked," she yelled through the door, getting ready to surprise.

Cake pushed open the door and was met with Maria teetering on stilts, wearing goggles and a paint smock, standing at her chest level, teasing her with a paint roller like a sword.

Dog lurched at Maria and barked. The Cake held her tight and told her to sit.

Maria dropped the pole and staggered backward, shocked. She fell against a heavy stair banister and hung on to save herself from crashing to the floor, crying.

Cake pulled the short leash and commanded the dog to sit while reaching for Maria and lowering her to sit on the second step. She hugged Cake's neck and sobbed out of fright.

"Okay, okay. Let's calm down. She thought you were going to hurt me. She's trained for that. Never scare her, or you may get shaken like a rag doll?" Unbuckling the stilts, she reassured Maria. "Zsa-Zsa will forgive you. You had better tell each other you're sorry."

Maria removed the goggles and held her hand flat to dog's nose. She wagged her tail and licked Maria's tears until she stopped crying.

Oceanna came to the door with Bob wondering what had happened; Maria was crying, and the dogs were barking. Stilts scattered. She checked Maria for scrapes and asked her to take dog and Bob into the kitchen for some peanut butter cookies. Maria took dog by the harness with Bob close behind and trotted off to eat and play in the basement clubhouse.

"How have you been? It's been about a week since we've seen you?" asked Oceanna.

"Looking for clues, and boy, did I get some," she felt herself blush. "How did you do in the storm? Half the city was blacked out. I drove by and saw a strange lavender light coming from the tower that night on patrol," said Cake, quickly changing the subject.

"Oh, crap. Come up to the tower and let me show you!" Reaching the sliding door, she gave Cake a warning glance and slid the door open. She gasped. The lavender mist covered the room and twinkled, floating gold sparks as fireflies fluttered all around the room.

She looked at Oceanna with disbelief.

"You should see this at night!" said Oceanna. "It is like another world. It makes you feel light-headed and . . . not unpleasantly strange if you stay long enough."

"This happened the night of the storm?" asked Cake as she stepped into the room.

"Yes! Yes, Viv and I were struck by lightning up here. The room exploded, we were knocked out, and when I came to . . .I thought Viv was dead, the place was covered with luminescent lavender mist. Whatever was in the herb jars blew up and covered the room. Who knows what all was in the concoctions? They mixed up and . . . magic?"

"Did you feel anything? Any effects, I mean?" asked Cake looking around the shelves, seeing the bats squeezing in and out of the beams. "Is that a glowing lavender pentagram pattern in the ceiling?"

"Yes! Strange!"

"Are you kidding?"

"No!"

"And am I seeing little purple bats in there with flashing gold eyes?" asked Cake, grimacing.

"Yes! Bizarre!" said Oceanna.

"Is this real?"

"Yes!" laughed Oceanna. "And there is more."

"You should call the police." Cake smiled.

"No! You're already here!" Oceanna dragged Cake by the arm over and pointed to the pentagon table in the middle of the room with an oversized leather-bound book on it, fizzling gold sparks and oozing lavender bubbles, labeled: 'Book of Sisters', in gleaming silver in-lay. Turning the cover open left some of the ooze on Oceanna's fingers.

The thick paper pages were hand-painted plates of each card of the Tarot.

"The Tarot is a deck of cards used to discern the future and look deeply into a person's internal and external life," said Oceanna, spreading the deck on the table. "A person can ask a question about something in their life, and the cards, in the hands of an expert, can be turned up in the order needed to give information. It's mystical, but the cards are often amazing. Insightful information, or a warning, maybe. There are two halves of the deck, the major and minor arcana. An experienced reader, like my grandmother, can become very sensitive and look into a person's life energy, becoming connected with the winds of fate or something like that. It's as ancient as the astrological practices."

"So, what does this mean? Your grandmother could read the future. Did she paint the cards into a book to develop a connection with them? Like meditating on them as she worked?" She spread out the cards to look more closely at each one. The intricate details and symbols with meaning.

"Maybe. She wrote detailed notations on the pages about what the cards offered and how to interpret them in readings. The Major Arcana can represent people. They can represent the person getting the reading. Representing the person in need. You pick from the deck and see what you get. It can lead the reading."

Shuffling the stack of cards of the Major Arcana, Oceanna spread them out face down and asked Cake to draw one.

She drew the Magician. Card number 1, Cake giggled.

Oceanna pulled one and turned it over, The Fool. They both laughed.

"I think the cards are reading us!" said Oceanna. "But look. The plates have photos of women stuck between them as though each woman had an identity for grandmother," she turned the page. "Look who is among them."

Cake lifted the photo stuck with plate number 6, The Lovers. "Is this Dolly Smack?"

"Much younger and much more colorful than the one we know today. Yes," said Oceanna. "And look who is sitting in the folds of The High Priestess pages. Grandmother Blanche."

"Are they witches?" asked Cake. "Were they a coven? Healers? Medicine women?"

Cake stared at the picture of Dolly, expressionless, and ran her fingers over the painted page, feeling the lavender slip over her fingers and tasting it. Mint.

"Dolly showed me some pictures of her days before and after dancing, one of you and Bob and your grandmother on a play swing together at about age four or five gave me some history of Bob senior's violent and cruel behavior, including the unhappy marriage and shared what happened to her husband. The deadly house fire blamed on Bob, never proven, and Bob's journey into and out of the hospital the other day. She gave me a cocktail with this strange lavender swirling in it, just like this stuff. It . . . affected me . . . mentally. I'll share the details another time, but . . . it makes me wonder."

"So, you think my grandmother was involved?"

"One way or another," said Cake. Her radio squawked a few code numbers that made her move.

"Vivian is on a selling trip, and I have Maria for a couple of days. Would you and Zsa-Zsa want to come over and have dinner tonight? We can discuss this, and I found more pictures," said Oceanna.

"Ya, about eight?" Cake nodded.

She headed to the door, down the stairs, and called dog. Maria clambered up the basement stairs behind her with Bob close behind. Maria handed her the leash.

"I filled her with cookies to apologize," said Maria, grinning.

"Great. See you tonight; this time, forget the stilts," said Cake as they hurried out the door.

BACKSTAGE

Ambition charged Vivian with energy as she set up her CozmetixX booth at the Fourth of July festival, on the grass, in the penetrating heat of the sun at Waterfront Park. The sun's rays infused Viv's body like a hot bath, rolling down through her bare shoulders and back, through her tan legs into her feet as she slipped through the cool grass. She tip-toed over the hot asphalt back and forth from the parking lot to the grass as she assembled her booth filled with products on display. She breathed in the smell of roses and river, filling the late morning air, shifting her mood from frantic to fun.

The stages were fluttering with red, white, and blue bunting. Concert production workers, almost finished with their final setups, wiped their brows, laughed, and got ready for the twelve hours of revolving stage changes over the three elevated sound stages.

Food trucks lined the park's perimeter, with acres of delicious offerings steam rolling out of their grill chimneys. Vendor booths offering products and trinkets, art and advice, clubs, and surprises stretched around the sides of the park for a mile. Aromas of meat roasting, wine, marijuana, and sweat floated in the air as the late morning grew into the afternoon, fans trundled in, and the music began to play.

Rainbow flags fluttered in the hot wind from the Hawthorn and Burnside Bridge's thick cement pillars marching across the wide Willamette River, welcoming everyone to come and commune. Grey steel Navy ships docked at the water's edge, setting sailors onto the grounds day and night for shore leave. Ladies of the evening trolled along the dock wall, offering fun and friendship to lonely sailors with cash in their dress-white pockets.

In the river floated vessels large and small anchored at the shore to experience the spectacle. Yachts with long white bows and tall masts bobbed to the beat of the drums, rocking to the blare of guitars and voices from noon to night. Kayaks, rowboats, small fishing boats, and canoes passed back and forth just beyond the crowded beach with passengers dancing, clapping, and waving scarves and sparklers.

Motorcycle clubs roared and rattled the air, twinkling their chrome down the streets, parking in perfect rows along the underpass' and rallying in the beer gardens, singing along. Belly dancers twisted and shook in gauzy puff pants and beads. Parents dragged their children in wagons. Transport vans lifted people in wheelchairs out onto the grass. The electric trains were jammed, spilling their crowds out, traveling from every burg.

With the first bang of the drum and the first guitar strum, the entire city of Portland was a circus. Tall buildings of glass and cement became party reverberators. The growl of soulful voices echoed off their brick surfaces, leaving pedestrians teetering among the notes. The festival fans ate until full, drank until dizzy, smoked without worry, then yelled and applauded for more.

Vivian's booth was a hit. Throngs of curious fans stopped and shopped through her wares. She had planned and filled three-ring binders full of examples of her mail-order options for the discreet purchasing of her Toys for Joys line. The CozmetixX colors and powders were demonstrated to people that wanted do-overs and beauty advice on-site. It drew looky-loos, fascinated by the transformations of customers in padded chairs admiring themselves in vanity mirrors set in the middle of the crowd. Customers were sold on the professional advice they saw Viv give during the makeovers, pulled out their wallets to pay in cash, and collected her pamphlets to shop from home. By the time the sun had set, she had packed what little did not sell, folded her booth, and stuffed it in the van. She felt proud and exhausted.

She strolled barefoot along the rows of booths, admiring the other vendors, a cup of micro vineyard wine in her hand, squeezing elbow to elbow, through the crowd to the stage Sunny would be playing on. Festival lights were strung on, around, and over the booths. Tiki torches fluttered in the evening breeze along the beach. The reflections shimmered yellow on the river's surface. The music rolled over the congregation, spinning them into dance.

A man with a long beard passed by Viv, handed her a joint and continued on his way, dissolving into the sea of passersby. She smoked what was left of it as she lolly-gagged along. The flavor of the smoke was strong, oily, and hot. The pupils of her brown eyes dilated. Halos and rainbows started to play in the lights. Floating among the spirits, she wound her way to the scaffolds of the center stage. Her mind expanded. She felt her body fill with heaven. The music became candy. Everything was funny.

Arriving at the stage stairs that trailed up to backstage catwalks, she flashed her pass and smiled at the security guard, who recognized her and let her in. She climbed the metal steps slowly, hanging onto the cool metal rail. She felt the tremble of people hurrying to get the band set up, shivering through her bare feet soles. She hesitated and closed her eyes, taking in the energy building up.

With the curtains closed, the band could arrange their instruments, drums, and mics and prepare mentally for their turn, a one-half-hour set, ending at 10 pm, when the fireworks would start. Vivian had never been backstage for a large event before. The anxiety and anticipation captivated her. A cold thrill ran up her spine.

Sunny stood in her red spotlight, making jokes at the grips guiding the lights. Several guitars were lined up on stands for quick changes. The drummer hit the skins now and then, chomping at the bit. Electricity fluttered from the pile of amplifiers stacked in the wings.

Viv stood behind the curtains, stage left, mesmerized by the hallucinated rainbow trails flowing from Sunny's black fender as she strummed it, polished and flashing. The curtains parted, and the announcer introduced them; the fans roared. Sunny Moon and the Satellites banged a blues beat, fried them with rhythm, stroked them with hard lyrics and Sunny's velvet voice.

High as a cloud, Viv's spirit soared over the rapturous throng, flew into the night sky, and discovered the connections between the stars and the meaning of life. Every breath was an adventure. Every movement is a dance. She felt her limits unravel. The world and its secrets were her playthings. Visualizing herself as a star, a virtual plan appeared in her mind.

At 10 pm, the Star-Spangled Banner was played by Sunny herself. The fuses were lit. Rockets shot from barges anchored offshore and sent bombs aloft, blasting in the sky. Popping and fizzling, sparks showered the city with color and smoke.

The stage quivered. Viv felt the blasts like she was riding them. When the fireworks were done, the crowd dropped their cups and filtered away, roaming to their cars, tired and filled with memories.

"Vivian, are you alright, honey? What did you get into?" Said Oceanna reaching down to collect her.

She was weeping. Curled up on the backstage floor. Dirt smudged her face. Tears trickled down her sunburned cheeks. Her eyes gleamed with wide pupils, black as the sky. She clung to Oceanna's collar, tired and misty.

"Dirty and out of your mind, you are still beautiful, darling. Let me take you home." She grinned and kissed her, pulled her to a stand, lifted her onto her back, carried her piggyback down the metal stairs, across the cool grass to the van, and home to bed.

CHAPTER 25:
LOLA CREEM AMONG THE JUNK

Lola talked to ghosts frequently, had no friends, and celebrated crowded holidays like July 4th, mostly alone.

"Ahh. Perfect night for a play date, right darling?" said Lola to the little girl's blackening body in the trunk while she drank and reclined in the wide back seat of a wretched '77 Lincoln Continental. The moon rose above the trees; stars returned to shimmer here and there across the night sky, cobalt blue to black. Beer iced in the cooler next to her on the floor. The built-in ashtray jammed with butts from her chain smoking. She chugged a cold one and threw the can out the missing sunroof, chuckling at the clatter it made when it hit another wreck a few yards away.

"I said, it's a perfect night for a date. And I called you, darling. I know you can hear me. This leather is not that thick," She mumbled and rolled over to face the back of the seat, speaking into it.

"I send you kisses, little girl. More than your family ever did. If it weren't for that power tower, Emerald Cake, I wouldn't have heard of anyone looking for you. You're mine now, sugar. I have you, kid!"

Pulling a long white cigarette from the pack in her breast pocket, she flipped her lighter, drawing a high flame, lit the tip, and shut the lid. She inhaled deeply and blew smoke rings that rose out the sunroof, wobbling and disappearing into the hot night.

"We can't do this on rainy nights; the leather is cracking. Stupid kids that run this place. Don't know what they've got. They don't appreciate the good stuff. Too busy running around like hellions, that tow motor roaring around," she said, clapping her hands together. "They don't make um like they used to. Not even ashtrays? There are no ashtrays in the new ones, child! Crap, it's all going to hell. Everybody's not an angel. Why do we all have to be perfect, no smoke, no drink, to hell with them," she folded her knees up into her chest.

Toxic gases lifted off of the greasy soil in the yard. Gooey sand, saturated from leaking engines and transmissions, burnt bearings, and gasoline contaminated with burnt rubber and metal flakes emanated unbreathable fumes. Her nose stung from the moldy fabric, causing her sinuses to drip. She wiped her nose on her sleeve. Dead things were hard to smell over the oil. Even dogs could fail to register the decay, figured Lola.

"Lady cop had all the questions. That is for sure. She had clues and questions and drew pictures of the place. I didn't see that one coming. I hadn't prepared for that one, child," she said, rolling onto her back and sticking her feet out the window.

She gripped the front seat headrests to pull herself to a sitting position. The leather upholstery squeaked under her weight. She looked out over the dark archers. Shadows of automobile hulks gave the fields a quiet, sinister texture, like stiff skeletons rooted to their spots, having given up the fight. Now and then, a rustle of rats or raccoons searching for food came from under a wreck. Lola abruptly pulled out her 38 Smith and Wesson and shot at the movement. The scratching stopped. She laughed.

"Oh no! I hope it wasn't your mother, darling," she smirked. Stubbing out one smoke and lighting another, she stared out into the yard. "Son of a bitch, this is Bob's fault. Again! He haunts me," she holstered her pistol, stood on the seat, and put her head out of the sunroof.

"It's the quiet ones that get you. Like you, darling. Yes. Like you. I love you, but you are dangerous. Bob knows the secrets of Lola Kreem, and I witnessed his. He watched them . . . you know. Doing it," she rubbed her eyes with her rough hands.

"Nurse Ambrosia. That's the other goblin that haunts me. The two of them. I can remember it like it was just happening now. Ambrosia gets close to Bob and puts him in the closet, drinking from her special cup. Gin, probably, but who knows what? She had access to the pharmacy. I didn't think that part through. Who knows what she had in her system before I dosed her? I dribbled it into her cup using a syringe, some clear stuff from bottles, I had snuck from the pharmacy when she had a date with one of the guards. It was an accident."

Plugging her ears and pulling her hair, she began to cry. Dropping out of the roof, she kicked the heavy door open with a grind, grabbed the cooler, drug it out of the limo, and rammed it down on the trunk lid.

"I didn't mean to kill her. She passed out and died in her own vomit right on the nurse's station counter. They couldn't revive her, but boy, they tried. Then the government guys showed up in a line of vans. Suspicious death of a nurse by overdose! Some of the staff said it was suicide. That got them off my trail. It was a surprise. They found lots of problems that got the shutdown. Yeah, it wasn't good. Little Bobby got to go home with the rest of them, finally. They should thank me. It was my dead nurse that shocked, um."

Lola's stomach growled and seemed to roll over. The tension in her shoulders stung from the knots brought on by her thoughts obsessed with her crime. Memories continued to flash in front of her. The more she tried to suppress them, the more they persisted.

"Crap! I loved Ambrosia; does that make me a dirty fag? She was a cheap whore! I never touched her. You're too young to know the aches and pains of being in the world, little girl. I have spared you from that, at least," she pulled out another cold beer, popped it, and drank it in one long gulp. "I tell you everything; I'm never saying it again."

She pulled her pistol from her holster and aimed the short chrome barrel under her chin. Pressing the barrel into her soft neck. She felt the metal roll against her neck as she swallowed and sweat. Standing for several minutes in the pitch dark, listening to the distant traffic swoosh along the ribbon of the highway below. She reminisced about a gentle day far in the past. One beautiful day, the last day she remembered ever playing free. A pretty child running with a kite, imagination sailing at the beach. Loving life in the sun, dreaming openly, existing gladly before the day the savage world collapsed upon her. Sighing, she lowered the gun, sliding it back onto her hip.

"Thanks for listening, darling! That's it! It's all a secret. All of it."

Shaking her heavy head, she patted the dusty trunk leaving fingerprints that she made sure to smear. She lifted the cooler and walked out into the pitch-black yard. An owl hooted close overhead, and the cat cried from far away. Fireworks blasted downtown. Sprays of color twinkled over the high buildings downtown, reminding her it was the Fourth of July.

Opening another beer, she sipped leisurely, circled the back ten acres on foot in the dark, threaded a serpentine trail among the sagging hulks, through the chain link gate, choked with thorny blackberries, back to the trailer, and passed out in her pristine kitchen.

C H A P T E R   2 6 :

THE CREEP AT THE GAZEBO

The moon peeped in and out of the clouds as a storm blew in. Leaves fluttered, twisting on tender stems until torn from their bushes, flying like lost kites into the night. The old paint canvases hung from the gazebo, creating Maria's shelter's walls. Pulling at the ropes as they fluttered, tugging but staying laced to each other, protecting her from the summer shower. Shadows bobbed over the sheets.

She poked at the dying coals in the metal fire pit in the middle of the gazebo. Oceanna had agreed to allow it as long as Bob was not given matches. After an afternoon of camping in the backyard, he had gone home to sleep in his own house and stuffing himself with his favorite hot dogs roasted over the fire on sticks. Maria was full and satisfied. She imagined Dream dozing, curled in her manger next to her, flipping her ears now and then to the one-sided conversation. The smoke hole in the roof let her look at the stars when the clouds parted.

She inhaled the soft fragrance of the smoke. Sighing and sleepy, she pulled her sleeping bag up to her chin. The urge for another last cigarette entered her thoughts. Her tobacco and papers were in the pocket of her cowgirl vest that hung at the front flap, along with the walkie-talkie, across from her bed. Debating whether she should bother, she watched Oceanna's silhouette cross the square of yellow light in the kitchen windows at the back of the house. Knowing she was there if needed made her feel cared for and close.

Oceanna's silhouette came and went like a puppet show. Maria provided the silly dialogue.

She argued with her cravings.

"More hot chocolate? Another smoke?" She mumbled as she considered the work to get the pot of water on the coals. She could drink from the used cup, even if it were sticky. They were her germs anyway. If she called Oceanna over the walkie-talkie, maybe she would bring out the hot chocolate, and they could talk for a while. She was good with the weird stories made up on the fly, and she always brought clean cups, which were preferred. Maria admitted to herself. She loved the rodeo, but she was not, herself, very rugged.

The sleeping bag zipper was sticking, making her fingers hurt as she tugged. Struggling to pull the sleeping bag open enough to escape through, she noticed the silhouettes on the canvas had changed. Oceanna was moving back and forth, then Vivian crossing from the kitchen to the living room. Sitting and standing and moving about, then there appeared a third shape. A shape popped up into the yellow square from below the window. A pointy head bobbed up and down, like someone peeping in the windows from the ground outside, very quietly, creeping.

"Dream! Crap! It's the creep! Quiet," she reminded herself. "We need to tell Anna. I don't think that creep knows we are in here."

Her hands shook and felt numb. The zipper kept jamming. She would have to crawl out like a snail from a shell. She had spent hours watching the snails undulate along the sidewalks; reflecting on their movements, she copied the rolling rhythms. Shedding the bedding, she touched her bare toes on the cold wooden floor, pressing gradually to find the boards that didn't squeak. Her lightweight lowered slowly and made less noise.

She discovered you could track, unheard, through almost any terrain if you were stealthy and slow.

Using the tip of her toes, clinging to the bunk, she lowered herself to the floor, her eyes focused on the movements on the canvas. She heard the click of a lighter and saw smoke shadows rolling up from the shape. Her heart pounded, and her knees felt weak. Her feet felt wooden, unable to move. She wondered if she would throw up the hot dogs and chili she had greedily consumed earlier.

"He is smoking and creeping! Wow. He is bad." Maria whispered to Dream, who lay still and alert, ears erect as she watched.

Maria rolled onto her belly and crawled to the door flap where the vest and walkie-talkie hung. Thunder rolled in the distance, giving her a noise cover enough to pop up and hide behind the door frame to reach them. The canvas door flapped open slightly with the breezes. Even though she had tied it in three places, there were gaps.

With one finger, she reached the gap and pulled it open slightly to ensure the threat was real.

"My eyes can play tricks on me; maybe I'm dreaming?" She thought. Making up adventures with sheriffs and bad guys was the center of her play most of the time. She considered there may be nothing there.

Shivering with fear, she peeked between the flaps. The motion lights flashed on and then off, but no one was there to see. Keeping her cheek pressed on the canvas, she lifted the walkie-talkie from its holster. It slipped out easily. Her hands tingled. She struggled to turn the "on" switch, but her fingers were numb. She fumbled weakly to grip the knob. It turned on. She held it to her chest and felt her heart pound.

"If the lights went on, something must have been there, right?" she whispered to Dream. "I didn't imagine that."

Drops of rain started to plop down on the roof and through the smoke hole into the fire, hissing as they flashed into vapor. Maria stood against the frame, working up her quivering guts to go out. She slowly stuck her feet into her boots and felt her ankle rub against her boot knife. She had forgotten she had it, having always carried it secretly, but had never brandished it. Sliding her fingers into the hidden sheath, she picked it out with two fingers, then smothered it in her sweating fist. The bone hilt fit into her palm perfectly. She carefully cut the ties to the door flap, braced herself, and counted.

"One . . . two . . . three." She leaped out, bursting through the flap onto the grass, knife raised, radio on in the other, shaking and shivering in a wide stance in her boots and underwear. The motion lights went on. No one was there. She remained still. The lights went off. She stayed still in the dark. Listening for footsteps. She wondered if Creep could still be hiding. The rain drizzled down, tickling her bare legs.

Then, the crash of a trash can lid hitting the ground rang out from under the stairs. The motion lights flashed on, and suddenly, the blur of a long, wild-eyed creature jetted from the darkness, yowling, and hissing. It bolted several yards from under the stairs, through Maria's legs, and into the darkness.

Maria stood, frozen to the spot. She lost the feeling in her arms. She thumbed the Morris Code button in a panic, with no understandable pattern. Her vision got fizzy. Her head spun. Before she collapsed into a dead faint, a stealthy figure in a thick overcoat with a hood covering a ghostly pale face ducked out from under the stairs and ran down the driveway in bare feet.

After Maria was revived and able to tell, she gave her story to Cake. Zsa-Zsa sniffed around the garden and found the only evidence of an intruder under the stairs: cigarette butts and a key, matching the one Maria wore around her neck. The missing second skeleton key to the original basement door locks leading to her clubhouse. It glowed faintly, a strange lavender light.

C H A P T E R   2 7 :

KIDNAPING

Ore week later:

Her thoughts were choppy, and her head hurt. Maria dreamed she was in a rodeo. She felt the muscled explosion of the bucking bull she straddled as it tossed its pointed horns and spun through the gate. She felt the hard landing of the hooves on the ground of the arena, pummeling her hips, her legs tied into a tight straddle. The angry beast snorted and moaned in anger, wild-eyed; it meant to kill her. Her fists were tied to its back with a stiff rope, crushing her fragile bones in a mad attempt to keep her there.

"Too tight!" she yelled. It's too tight! You're breaking my hand!"

Yanking hard, she could not get free. Her limbs felt rubbery. She was unable to jump off the beast. She heard a familiar voice tell her to stop struggling, followed by a hard slap across her face. Her face felt numb. Then movement, like the roll of bus wheels pulling out from a stop and driving down a road. She heard traffic noises, other cars and the roar of a bus engine near her, and the familiar rattles of the short bus that transported Bob to and from his job.

Confused and dizzy, she slowly came to and realized she was right. She was duct-taped to the spare wheelchair Lola kept in the yellow outlined spot reserved for passengers in wheelchairs, directly behind her driver's seat on the bus.

When she could raise her spinning head, she could see the street, cars going in the opposite direction on the two lanes of Stark Street. Her stomach felt sick, and her mouth was dry but not gagged. Her wrists were taped to the armrests, and her feet were taped to the footrests. She wiggled her fingers and toes that tingled. Sweat drizzled down her sides. She sweats with frustration, anxiety, and the heat of a ninety-nine-degree August day.

She shook her head, fighting to get through the fog in her mind. Trying to get free, she twisted her wrists and rolled her feet, stretching the plastic tape. The heat of the sun radiated in, softening the glue. She felt the adhesive slip, mixing with the moisture on her skin.

Lola smirked, watching Maria in the long rearview mirror while maintaining her usual safe speed and observation of the traffic rules. She was not in a fuss. For Maria, it was an ugly calm.

"Hello, Maria! What's up? Are you comfortable?" asked Lola.

"What are you doing?" asked Maria, coming out of her daze.

She worked carefully. Feeling imperiled, her instinct kicked in. Focusing on escaping, she figured she could jump out the back emergency door if she got loose. Lola had shown her how to use the side wheelchair lift and taught her how to use the emergency exits when she rode with Bob to work. She was not supposed to give undesignated people rides, but Bob's mother had authorized her as a helper, so giving Maria rides now and then could be accepted. Maria realized she might have been planning to trap her all summer.

"You're okay, Maria. I'm gonna take care of you from now on. It's okay."

"If it's okay, why am I tied? This is nuts!" Her stomach hurt, and she spit on the floor. "I feel sick."

"Oh, that's from the medicine I gave you."

"What medicine did you give me?" I don't take medicine."

"So, you would sleep, and I could get you home. In the soda pop, I put it in there. It's a hot day; you are thirsty out, galloping around. Bam! I got you," said Lola.

"I have a home with my dad. I don't need another home," she muttered and started to cry.

"Where the hell is he? Your dad is never there, Maria. It's not safe, as you can now see. Bad people can hurt you if you are not careful," she checked, the traffic lights turning yellow.

"I thought you were a good person. You take guys like Bob to work and all that," said Maria hoping to get on Lola's good side and get set free.

"To hell with little Bobby and all the rest of them. I'm just a survivor, like you."

"Are you the peeping tom? Creep! I feel sick," yelled Maria, her stomach turning.

Lola slammed her hands on the steering wheel several times, as hard as she could, flailing her arms. "I am the boss now. I'm taking care of things. I'm not complaining! I'm taking charge!"

Officer Cake and Zsa-Zsa were patrolling down Stark Street. At the same time, Cake talked to a dog in the usual manner, adding up clues and unraveling conflicting evidence, when she noticed the transport bus number 1313, with Lola driving towards her. She was surprised to see Lola flailing her arms at the wheel. Cake waved at her, checking for things to be alright, but she didn't notice or wave back. The Cake took her foot off the gas pedal.

As they passed each other, Cake noticed a dark head of hair on the driver's side in the wheelchair spot, and the hair parted at the back of the head like Maria wore with her long pigtails. She knew Maria sometimes rode with Bob on the bus, but that was earlier in the day, and she never rode in the reserved spot behind Lola. She turned the wheel toward Maria's block to see if she could find her.

Circling back ten blocks, they cruised through the usual streets Maria would be found playing on, galloping, looking for roadkill and the elusive Maine Coon that kept her on patrol. It appeared and disappeared, keeping Maria on the lookout. Cake fingered the walkie-talkie code button to signal she was in the neighborhood. No return signals.

When they got to Maria's house, her father's truck was not there. Cake pulled up in front of the house and pulled Zsa-Zsa out on the short leash. The dog understood it was time to work and sniffed the familiar sidewalk, smelling for her friend. Cake knocked but no answer. The house was quiet. The camper was in the driveway. Cake checked it for signs of Maria playing horse ranch or having an imaginary campout.

Zsa-Zsa barked at a spot under the front rose bushes. It was Maria's walkie-talkie, still turned on, and the junior sheriff badge Cake had pinned to her vest, scattered, and slightly covered with mulch like someone tried to hide them in a rush. She left the evidence where it lay, hurried the dog into the cruiser, turned the wheel, and headed for Lola's trailer.

CHAPTER 28:

MARIA AND LOLA STRUGGLE AT THE YARD

Maria continued to roll her wrists and ankles, loosening the tape that bound her out of Lola's line of sight. Having polished her leather boots daily, the leather was supple, and her father had purchased them half a size too large to give her room to grow, so she had to wear socks to fill in the gaps. She found the sloppy fit handy. The sloppy fit was letting her feet slip out gradually. The sheath of her boot knife moved up the boot, exposing the hilt at the top brim. Slowly her vision cleared to a greasy blur, and her thinking started to sharpen.

"Where are we going? You said you were taking me home," ventured Maria.

"Heh. I'm taking you to my house, and we will have a little party," said Lola, gingerly stopping at a light, preparing for it to turn green.

"I already had a birthday party. And I don't want a party with you."

"Listen, Maria, little girl, you are not being raised well by your father. I drive by your house every day, and his big bad truck is never there. And he leaves you to be raised by a retarded man and crazy dykes, living in a witch's house! So . . . I am gonna save you the pain of how being neglected turns out! Why wait for the chips to fall, baby? Heh! I'm gonna spare you the trouble and kill you myself."

Lola glared back at Maria with a hard stare. The light turned green, and just as she moved into the intersection, a car ran the light, causing Lola to jam on the breaks, lurching the wheelchair forward, sinching the seat belt around Maria's chest and diaphragm forcefully, driving out a fountain of vomit from her mouth, spattering the floor and windshield with half-digested tortillas and eggs.

Lola felt the jerk in her chest as the shoulder belt cut across her neck. She screamed at the vomit spray now covering the dashboard, door, and floor mats.

"I'm gonna scrape that up and make you eat it like they do in juvenile detention!" She winced to think about the evidence she would have to clean up with her special strategy of baking soda and vinegar scrub with a bleach wash for children's messes like this. It was always best to keep a clean surface in case of nosey visitors like Officer Cake and her mutt.

"I'd like to choke her and beat that K-9 with its own tail," said Lola. "I must do a very good job hiding this from your bitch friends, Maria! Officer Cake and her mutt. Zsa-Zsa. What kind of alien name is that?"

"She is German! Stupid! That is a German name for a beautiful girl."

"Don't call me stupid ever again!" Lola made it through the intersection and paid close attention to the rules of the road. She didn't need a good samaritan to try to assist her or follow her now. If a cop tried to help, how could she explain a historical client taped to a wheelchair, in four-point restraints, with projectile vomit dripping off the windshield? She stayed in the right lane, letting cars cross in front of the bus like a polite motorist.

Without taking her eyes off the road, she pulled a short bat with a curved handmade handle out from under her duffel bag behind her seat and smacked the leg rest of the wheelchair with a crack, just missing

Maria's knees. She had designed its length and shape to hit the passenger's shins behind her just below the knee, crippling the child or torturing her, whatever they deserved. She could discourage outbursts with little effort and never take her eyes off the road.

Maria recoiled at the sound of the bat striking the metal and knew Lola could have broken her skinny knee if she had made contact. The sharp lurching forward stretched the tape around her wrists, and the heat was softening it by the minute; a few inches more, and the knife should be in her grasp. Her mind was returning to her. The smell of vomit cut through her nostrils. Her heart pounded while she thought about how to kill Lola with her bare hands before Lola gave up. She had nothing to lose now.

Her father would save her if he could. He was very brave. Cowboys talked about him behind his back because he was only five foot two, one hundred and thirty-five pounds. She heard them when it was his turn to mount, but she had faith in his virtues, tight muscles, and big heart. She considered herself to be like him now; she would have to prove it. Lola probably underestimated her like the cowboys did her father. She was so small.

"This is my advantage," she thought. "This time being small is better. Small feet, small hands . . . big fight!"

She loosened her feet, sliding her heels up, pointing her toes, ready for a surprise leap, with her feet hidden by the boots. She mustered her strength as Lola made the left turn into her driveway and lolled the nose of the bus into the rear of the driveway, near the back of the trailer, hiding the door from view.

Lola turned off the engine and pulled on the parking brake with a thud. She opened the accordion front door and examined the barf mess before leaving her seat. She reached into her duffel bag, pulled out a vile of medicine and a small syringe, stuck them in her breast pocket, unbuckled her seat belt, and looked at Maria in the rearview mirror.

It was deadly quiet without the engine roaring. Even the junkyard was quiet. Traffic on the street, 300 hundred feet behind them, sounded like water rushing off rocks. Lola pulled up her pant leg to check her gun in the ankle holster, pulled it out for Maria to appreciate, spun the bullets in the wheel, returned it to the holster, and got out of her seat.

Shooting Maria on the bus was impossible, thought Lola. The mess would be too much to clean. She had to get Maria out into the yard. She had to ensure she was ready for a fight, like bathing a cat. Maria would be a squirmer.

Estimating Lola's next move, she would not shoot in the bus. She was going to give her a shot, make her sleep. She flattened her hands to yank out from the tape, readied her feet on her tiptoes, and braced herself for Lola's weight to land on her.

"Well, Maria, darling. We are at the crossroads," she pulled a menthol from a pack in her bra and talked with it bobbing up and down in her lips as she spoke.

"Hey, I need a smoke too. I roll my own, but I would settle for one of yours."

"You are a little girl. Since when do you smoke?" Lola lit the smoke and coughed.

"It's better than the chew like my dad does. His spits and his teeth are brown. I smoke with Bob all the time!" she said. "I'm feeling shaky in this crazy situation, and it would calm me down! At least you could give me a last smoke! Like the movies," she started to cry, tears dripping down her sweating cheeks. She bowed her head down, hiding her defiant expression.

Lola sucked her smoke and removed the vile and the syringe from her pocket, filled the syringe with a yellow liquid drawn from the vile, put the needle cover back on, and put it in her pocket again. Watching Maria cry softened her stance slightly. It would help if Maria were more relaxed. Maybe being friends by sharing would be a good move, considered Lola.

"Okay, Maria. You're a good kid. I really like you and want to be friends. I'm gonna light you a smoke, but if you struggle, I'm gonna hit you with the medicine hard. If it puts you to sleep or kills ya . . . it's up to you," she gave a slight grin. "I'm an expert on giving this stuff. I haven't missed yet."

Maria raised her face and looked at Lola, watching her body, examining her expression. She nodded. "Okay," she whispered, her heart pounding.

Lola tapped out another menthol, put it into her own mouth, and lit the tip. She bent over Maria, leaning on the armrest, and carefully approached Maria's crusty lips with the filter end. Maria yanked her left hand free of the tape, reached the hilt of her knife, and clutched it; she slammed the blade through Lola's hand, burying it deep into the armrest, pinning her there. Lola shrieked as a fountain of her blood sprayed up into their faces.

Giving a warrior's yell, Maria pulled her feet from her boots and kicked at Lola's knees, hoping to cripple her, hoping to give herself time to run out of the bus's front door and get to the street before Lola could stand.

Working the seat belts with slippery blood-drenched latches slowed her in freeing her chest. Lola socked Maria in the face. Maria punched her in the nose and pulled her hair, getting herself to a stand. Lola reached for her gun, but Maria kicked her knees, keeping it out of reach.

Fumbling for the anesthetic syringe in her breast pocket gave Maria an advantage of a few seconds. Lola had one chance to stick it; she had to get it into her neck the first time. Blood had already filled her pocket, making the syringe hard to hold. The cylinder was thin, the needle was fragile, and Maria was bucking. If she got shot in, Maria would drop into a comma in seconds; she could be dragged off and shot later.

Maria tore the tape and seat belts away, got to her feet, and slid on her own bloody socks. Lola pulled the cover off the needle with her teeth, jammed Maria in the neck, and rammed the plunger down, filling her with drugs.

"Creep! I hate you!" yelled Maria, spinning like a wild mare, an enraged gleam in her eyes. She kicked Lola in the gut and stumbled down the steps. Sliding in a pool of blood, face down onto the gravel driveway on her belly, she crawled under the bus and passed out.

CAKE AND ZSA-ZSA AT THE YARD

Cake had to write a ticket for a motorcycle that ran a red light, delaying her arrival at Lola's. She turned on the flashers as she pulled into the driveway. The look of the bus parked at an odd angle, doors open with no one in sight, was suspicious. She pulled the cruiser diagonally, blocking Lola's escape. She scanned the area visually. She knew Lola had a gun and didn't want to err on the side of getting hit with it.

"No kid in a wheelchair rolling around. What the hell? Okay, girl, let's get the vests, " Cake said, moving into action.

Letting Zsa-Zsa out, the dog gave a hard shake. She felt the nervous energy and sniffed and huffed with excitement. She knew who to look for. Cake fastened the Velcro straps around the dog's chest and belly. The new bulletproof vests covered more of her were thicker than last year's model and had a gold badge with her name stenciled on the sides.

Leaving the doors open for protection, Cake pulled her gun and stayed low. The dog crouched next to her. She called out to Lola over the megaphone.

"Lola! It's Officer Cake! We are here to help. Are you alright?" she tried to present Lola as a victim, hoping to enlist her cooperation. No callback. No movement. Dog growled and huffed.

Cake scanned the front door of the trailer. No signs of trouble there. Then she looked more closely along the side of the bus and noticed blood smeared along it and a bloody handprint on the glass door. She called out again. No reply or movement. Staying low. Bending, they stepped carefully toward the front of the bus. Blood-soaked socks lay crumpled on the gravel, and a pool of blood dripped down the stairs. Cake braced herself and gave the dog the signal to go.

Zsa-Zsa jumped up the bloody stairs and began searching. Cake covered her rear. No windows in the back of the trailer from which Lola could shoot. She followed the dog up the stairs, sickened at the amount of blood on and around the wheelchair, plastic tape wrapped around the arms, and red cowgirl boots still tied onto the foot pieces. Vomit on the floor and windshield. Cake quickly put together what must have happened. Maria's secret boot knife, jammed in the armrest with a piece of someone's flesh hanging from it, maybe the sign of what sealed her fate. Now dog's feet were soaked with gore.

"Seek! Dog, seek!" commanded Cake.

The dog ran past her, down the stairs, slipping, and followed a sent to the overgrown junk yard fence the trailer abutted and barked at the tangled gate. A small engine sputtered to a start on the other side of the fence, hidden by thorn bushes. The vines stuck in the dog's muzzle and whipped around her face threatening to blind her. She could not break through.

Rushing to find another lead, she sniffed an old ladder that leaned against the tool shed. Curling her paws around the worn pegs, dog clung onto the worn rungs. The old wood rattled as she picked her way, climbing to the shed's roof. Springing on her hind legs, she paused a moment gathered her strength and jumped, sailing over the four-foot gap between the shed roof and the trailer top. The only way into the yard was the vault over the ragged thorns, and hope to land safely, not knowing what would be on the other side.

Zsa-Zsa ran in a circle several times to gain momentum, then sprung as far as she could into the air just as Cake looked up to see her pass over her head. A shot rang out from the other side. The Cake called for backup, climbed the ladder, jumped the four-foot gap to the trailer, took a couple of long strides from the front to the rear, and bound into a flying leap over the thorns. As she hurled herself over the bushes, she saw a dog chasing an old circus surrey with a red and white striped canvas roof, dragging the tailpipe that sputtered blue smoke, heading out across the yard in the direction of the far end of the lot, near the freeway.

The Cake landed on her buttocks, bouncing on the flat roof of a 50's metro van. She slid on the wide windshield, rolled down the glass, and fell into the greasy mud, knocking her head on the front bumper. The pistol is still in hand.

Shaken but not injured, Cake ran in hot pursuit. Taking the shortest route, she leaped over hulks with long, wide strides, like an elk, easily clearing the hoods of sinking classics while picking her path through scrap piled along the way. She fired a warning shot, letting Zsa-Zsa know she was coming.

Lola's left hand bled through the rag she had tied around it. Steering the sagging surrey was not easy. It bounced on weak suspension and bobbed threw mud puddles on flattening tires. Maria leaned and flopped on the bench seat beside her, tired and disoriented, falling onto Lola's shoulder for stability.

The surrey reached a short wooden bridge that passed over an oily pond fed by a trickling stream. Zsa-Zsa caught up and sprung up into the rear of the cart. Lola shoved the drunken girl off the bench seat into the pond just as the dog sank her teeth into Lola's back. She shot two rounds into dog, spinning her from the cart into the pond as well.

Pressing the gas to the floor, she rattled her way to the furthest acre nearest the freeway. She had prepared the escape by cutting the chin links for an opening large enough for the surrey to go through, planning to ride down the bike path and disappear into a drainage culvert. She found the opening blocked by an old VW combi-bus, with the word "sold" painted on the side, recently deposited there.

Cake strode up close behind and slid to a stop at the bridge when she saw Zsa-Zsa, clinching Maria's collar in her teeth, yanking mightily to pull her from the putrid tar of the creek that threatened to absorb them both. Grabbing the handle on the back of the vest while the dog had Maria, she hauled them free, with a sucking sound, like pulling a cork from a bottle. She noticed the glint of two rounds stuck in the Kevlar of dog's vest, right on the heart. No blood on the dog or Maria, who was coming back to consciousness.

"Stay with Maria! Stay Zsa-Zsa! Good girl, I have her," she patted her head. The dog gave a sloppy tail wag in agreement, and Cake returned to her pursuit.

Maneuvering carefully, staying low, and moving quickly, she crept closer to Lola's surrey. She scanned the physical situation. Lola was pushing the bus back and forth, rocking it to push it out of the way to get access to the cut chain links. She had cut a gap large enough for any activity that may call for a back door approach.

As Cake approached, Lola shot a round in her direction. It ricocheted off the hood of the black limousine and rang off at a right angle into a barrel full of a greasy slop of trash, oil, and gas. It began to smoke and then flamed.

Cake tip-toed up along the side of the limo swung open the thick front passenger door and crouched behind it as a shield. She knew she would be safe from any fire from Lola; the metal door could withstand a bazooka, thought Cake. She lay across the front seat and pulled her feet off the ground. The windshield was covered with grime she could use as camouflage. Peeking up over the dashboard to catch Lola's location and stance, she waited.

Lola gave up rocking the bus and crawled into it, hoping to squeeze through the sliding door giving her cover and access to the fence, then escaping on foot down to the bike path and the freeway. When cops figured out she was gone, it would be too late.

She slithered through the window, grabbed the sliding door handle, and pushed. The pressure nailed her foot through the rotten floorboards. The rusty metal bit into her calf like a bear trap, setting off a miserable howl that made Cake's skin crawl. Trapped, she raised her gun and scanned the yard. She shot wildly at any movement, including the face behind the windshield of her favorite limo, shattering it.

Glass fragments showered down on Cake, then all was quiet, except for the huff and puff of the little surrey's sick two-stroke engine, still idling.

Billows of black smoke from the trash fire wafted, blowing across the yard between Cake and Lola, obscuring their vision, and polluting the breathable air.

Using the smoke as cover, Cake crawled to the fence and crouched, positioning her several feet from the flat nose of the bus. She could see the top of Lola's scalp and hear her rustling, maybe trying to reload.

"Lola Kreem, It's Officer Cake. Throw out your gun and come out!" She yelled through the missing glass in the windshield.

"To hell with you! I'm not giving up! Come and get me, you green-eyed devil!" yelled Lola as she stuffed an old towel, she found in the trash on the bus between her bleeding calf and the sharp metal gnawing into her flesh. She stayed silent. Unable to get free, left-hand bleeding, she clutched the gun in her right and aimed toward Cake's voice through the windshield. If Cake put her head up, she could shoot her in the face, disabling her, then she would have time to free her leg and limp out the fence, she thought. It might take hours for the cops to figure it out.

"What's the point now, Lola? The girls will be found," yelled Cake.

"Here is the point, Rah-Rah! Who takes care of the little girls? All the bull about caring for the vulnerable. Maria? Father was gone most of the time, so she is babysat by a retarded man, with a vampire for a mother, who murdered his father in a house fire and a couple of lezzy witches? Tell me, Cake, what happens to little girls on the street? I took care of them before bad guys could get them," she fired a shot in Cake's direction, thinking maybe she'd get lucky and hit her.

Slinking low around the side of the bus, Cake knelt at the fence at the rear. Lola shooting out the front, let her know she was unnoticed and hidden. She could see the back of Lola's head in a rearview mirror and the blood dripping from Lola's shoe under the bus.

"I took care of them at the stupid asylum! Bob Smack was treated like a hero for surviving the hell hole, but I had to hide in the back. My dead nurse. I killed Ambrosia! It was the best accident I ever had! Cops saw the nightmare going on in there! They could ignore hundreds of dead patients but a dead nurse? That was a big deal. Her death, an apparent overdose, I was free too. There were so many sloppy deaths around there; I was never questioned. I have had nightmares ever since."

Cake sprung up, stuck her gun through the missing rear glass, and aimed at Lola's chest, surprising her, less than ten feet away.

"Stop and drop your gun, Lola. It's over. Don't move."

Lola stuck her gun's muzzle under her chin and froze, tears streaming down her cheeks.

"If you give up now, I will testify for you, and you could go to a psychiatric facility rather than jail. Think about it," said Cake, unsure if that would help or hurt.

For a minute, neither one moved. Memories played in Lola's mind. Helpless ghosts suffered before her stinging eyes. She heard faint sounds of sirens like a baby's cry in the distance as a line of squad cars sped down the freeway in their direction, and the beat of a news helicopter's blades popped ever closer.

"You've got me there, Officer Cake. You have me there. Going back to the loony bin?" She rotated her shoulders to face her. "I guess I never left."

When her own bullet passed through her head, the force rocked her body, but because her leg was stuck to the floor, she stayed upright, weaving wildly back and forth like a crazy inflatable Bobo Clown, punching back. It exploded her skull, splattering her brains into Cake's face and the entire bus interior. The back of her skull, scalp, and hair launched out the sunroof, tangling on the chain link fence, hanging like a macabre dreamcatcher.

For this, Cake and Zsa-Zsa received; a medal of honor from the governor, a hero's accolades, an invitation to be the next Grand Marshals at the Gay Pride Parade and haunting nightmares of her own.

C H A P T E R   3 0 :

VIVIAN LEAVES FOR AUSTIN

"**Y**ou're leaving? Tonight? For Texas?" cried Oceanna.

"It's a business decision! I want to permanently get the name of Vivian Lash CozmetixX and Toys for Joys into the entertainment market. That's where the money is. Right? You know this." said Viv, as she sorted through her wardrobe, packing the trunks with her most flattering outfits.

"I feel used! You used me to get closer to Sunny and Kelly, and now you're following them on their tour around the states, and hint, hint, flirting with anyone you think will help your career. I thought you loved me and . . ."

"I do love you, and I have loved our time, but I have to grow, Anna! Don't limit me! I have given you all I have to give you! Right now, Asian is in, and the camera loves me. I have to strike while the iron is hot." said Viv, carefully inventorying her makeup and packing them into a square CozmetixX makeup case.

She hesitated to appreciate the dramatic reflection in her dressing mirror of Oceanna crying, naked, and flopping out among the tousled sheets on the bed. Side tables were busy with scattered remains of the night, champagne glasses smeared with lipstick, ashtrays full of butts, and candles flickering with her sobs.

"You are beautiful in heartbreak, Anna," said Viv feeling the tug of regret on her heartstrings.

"And you are cruel in your beauty, Viv!" she kicked her feet and rolled onto her stomach.

Slamming the lid shut, she snapped the latches hard and crossed the room to the bed.

"I do love you, in my way," said Viv to the back of Oceanna's head. "Look at me. Look."

"No! Take your crap and leave! You like to see me cry over you. I don't want to watch this disappearance, Viv. Just go," she turned her face into the pillows and covered herself with a sheet.

Viv removed her robe and lay naked on Oceanna's back, reaching under her, cupping her breasts, and hugging her.

"Let's just love and let go and feel good about what we have enjoyed, Anna. Why not feel the sweetness and live realistically? I have to follow the course of my life. It now goes to Austin and music. It's my creative journey," she whispered into Oceanna's ear, wet with tears, and kissed it. Oceanna sighed and did not pull away.

"This is not fair. I'm attached to you, Viv! I feel abandoned. I am suffering with you leaving me; you must understand that!"

"Yes, I understand that. But I have to follow my dream and create on a different level. Our lives crossed, and we fell into each other wonderfully," she slowly pulled the sheet from between their bodies and felt Oceanna's heat soak into her belly. "You're exciting and strong and beautiful and loyal, and did I say exciting?" she brushed Oceanna's messy hair back out of her face. "Look at me."

"No fair! You know I can't resist you," she untangled their legs, rolled onto her back, and looked into Viv's dark almond eyes.

"Listen, I'm going to make love to you again, babe. I'm going to show you how I feel again. I'm going to taste you and be inside you and put you inside me until we scream," Viv kissed her softly on her pouting lips. "Then, you will help me finish packing and take my stuff to the car, and we will cry, say goodbye, and I am leaving. And we are going to love life just the way it is. Are you ready?"

Two hours later, Oceanna shoved the last trunks into the CozmetixX van, crying and packing her lover up obediently. The street was silent; houses were dark. The September night breezes felt like velvet; stars twinkled obliviously.

"I'm going to kiss you twelve times, once for each fabulous month of our romance," Viv whispered through tears. Oceanna laughed and received delicious kisses twelve times. Then, Viv got into the driver's seat, started the motor, and pulled away. As Oceanna stood barefoot and broken in the middle of the street, watching her disappear around the corner, the van coughed and gave a sharp backfire.

Two months later:

The door was locked when Vivian returned to Portland unexpectedly on Halloween night. Oceanna's Jack-o-Lanterns were carved and lit. Soft flames fluttered inside, giving ghoulish grins life. Bats fluttered in the eaves of the tower, peeping as they consumed moths drawn to the holiday lights strung along the windows. The old porch was decorated with flashing orange lights and plastic spiders poised on gauzy webs stretching across the front door. A large wooden bowl of candy bars sat out as an offering to Trick or Treaters warding off tricks while Oceanna and her band of monsters were haunting the neighbors. She clutched her leather vest around her.

From her stance on high stairs looking out over the street, Viv squinted to see if she could find them. Large pumpkins lollygagged on front stairs up and down the street. Children and their parents knocked and sang for the doors to open, and bags were held out for rewards. She saw Maria's father's truck parked in front of their place.

The assault on Maria and Officer Cake's capture of Lola Kreem and her heroic K-9 had made the national news, so Viv was surprised to see any celebration adorn her home. But maybe moving on was the point of any party. It looked like Ralfie might be in. She went to the front door and knocked.

Red lights flashed in the eye sockets of a life-sized skeleton hanging in a tree, and the blood-curdling howl of a werewolf came from a speaker in the bushes. The door flew open, and a small man in a savage wolf mask, wearing nothing but shredded sweatpants and black fake fur glued to his otherwise hairless shoulders, roared at her. She jumped back and nearly fell off the steps. He grabbed her arm in time to keep her on her feet.

"Oh, wow, Vivian? Is that you? Or is it just a pretty disguise?" said Ralfie pulling off his mask. His wide tobacco-stained smile seemed to glow from his dark, ruggedly handsome face, framed by two long back braids of hair tied with leather thongs and small black feathers, which he always proudly wore.

"Tribesman! What the hell are you doing? Trying to kill the kids?" she sputtered breathlessly, clutching her large purse.

"Hey! How did you recognize me?" he laughed, pulling the door open, inviting her in.

"You have always been a wolf in cowboy's clothing, Mr. Brava," said Viv, happy to be invited out of the cold.

"Where is everybody?" she asked.

"They are out in costumes messing up the streets, right? Yah! Lots have been going on around here. Let's talk. Want a beer?"

He tossed his mask off and stepped outside to see if any kids were coming. Trick or Treat was coming to a close. He blew out the jack-o-lanterns, turned off the decorations, closed the door, and dimmed the lamp lights.

"Hey, where's your fancy van? What happened?" He offered her a seat on the leather couch and went to the refrigerator for a beer. She plopped onto the cushions, dropped her purse on the floor, and began crying.

"The engine blew up halfway back, somewhere in Nevada. I had to leave all my inventory in the van, wait hours for a tow truck to take me to a shop, and get a rental. The best I could do was a small moving truck. I have been driving for days. I'm tired, beat, and starving."

Popping open two bottles of beer, cradling a bottle of tequila and lime in his arm, he returned from the kitchen, handed a beer to Viv and, climbed onto the other end of the couch cross-legged, then gave her a short smile and a red bandana from around his neck to dry her tears.

"What the hell happened to you? Your confidence is messed up," said Ralfie.

She kicked off her red high heels and landed her feet up on the coffee table.

"I went too far. My timing was off. My suggestions weren't accepted. The star of the band, Sunny Moon felt distracted," she pulled a long drink from the beer. "It's smooth. Thanks."

He unfolded a pocketknife, carved a couple of wedges from the lime, turned the cap from the tequila, took a swig, bit the lime, and grimaced against the burn.

"Ya? That's all? What else? You are a hot saleslady, right? The stuff you sell is good. Seems strange they would dump you," he said.

"I need the strong stuff if we are gonna talk about my greatest failure," she reached for the bottle but refused the lime and took a swig. She laid her head back and let the warmth of the medicine soak in.

He packed a short pipe with a sticky marijuana bud, pressed a lit stick match into it, and sucked in the fragrant smoke.

"I got lost. Got out of balance, off my strengths. I tried to push rather than draw them in. I felt confident and ready when I left and then when I got down there and tried to fit in and become . . . needed. I think they felt uncomfortable that I left Anna. She is their friend. And I guess it's not good to flirt with the manager. I just wanted in! My looks have always helped me," she reached down and dug through her purse, pulled out a small compact mirror, and checked her face. Her mascara was smudged, and her lipstick was gone; her eyes felt gritty, and her hair was windblown.

"Can I use your bathroom? I need to freshen up. Can I borrow a tee shirt?" she groaned.

"Oh, yeah! Yes, please do. The towels in the cupboard are clean; shower if you want. I turned up the water heater, so the hot is hot."

He took another pull on the pipe and handed it to her. She took a drag, picked up her purse, and nodded as she went down the short hall. He put on a soft jazz radio station and started a fire in the fireplace against the chill.

She left the bathroom door ajar, feeling the need for neighborhood updates.

Ralfie leaned on the wall in the hall, telling her what he knew.

"Maria is in counseling now. She is strong like her father. She cries at night sometimes from bad dreams like that, but she will make it okay. I stay home more now. Take it easy a bit. They have asked her to talk to the other schools about what happened. It's part of the "in vivo" thing they do for healing trauma. Officer Cake and her dog go around with her."

"How's Anna doing? Is she . . . seeing anyone that you know of?" Clouds of steam rolled into the hall as Viv splashed around. She turned off the water, grabbed a towel, put her hair in a turban, and pulled on his T-shirt that smelled like aftershave.

"Oh, I know you would be a hard act to follow, Viv. I know Anna loved you all the way."

The only person coming around is that officer; that's it. That's all."

She yanked open the door and gave him a stare. "Who is it? Is she getting to know the giant cop? Crap. She's pretty hot."

"They've been doing stuff with Maria and Bob. Fixing the house and all that," he shrugged.

She stomped to the couch, plopped down, and lit a cigarette.

"I've gotta process this. I need another drink," she said, stretching out on the couch.

"Settle down. You're unforgettable, right?" He stuffed a large bud into the pipe, took a hit, and handed it to Viv, who dramatically sprawled out, stretching her legs across the cushions. She drew hard, closed her eyes, and held it, then released a blue smoke slowly.

Ralfie slid onto the other end of the couch and took her bare feet into his lap. Gathering them into his hands, he admired the softness of the pale skin against the brown leather of his hands. He petted her ankles and cupped her heels in his thick palms, slowly running his thumbs into her arches. Pressing his fingertips between her toes, he admired the shine of the red gloss polish on her well-manicured nails. She smelled like flowers. He rolled his fingers along the top of her foot and stroked up her calf to her knee, loosening sore muscles skillfully. She moaned. He drew her foot to his face, put her toes into his mouth, and rolled his tongue between them.

CHAPTER 31:

FIRE ON HALLOWEEN

Maria clomped ahead of Oceanna and Bob up the short brick path to the last porch on their trick-or-treat haunt, decorated with a giant orange spider with flashing eyes and blue fangs. She dressed as a vampire cowgirl with red cowgirl boots, authentic black and white calfskin chaps, her large silver rodeo belt buckle, six guns on each hip that fired real caps, her red fringed vest, and new, real steel Hero's badge, and glow in the dark fangs. She inhaled the fresh air, checked the weight of the bag of candy she was hauling, looked up at the stars, and felt a soft hint of joy.

Her muscles ached after the karate class every other day, but the soreness reminded her of her new strength and girl power. Cake had taught her some extra holds that made her feel like a ninja, and Zsa-Zsa had become her best animal friend after Dream and Bob.

Wearing herself out to the point of exhaustion had become the way to go to sleep. Sit-ups, jumping jacks, and standing crouches were faithfully done every night, one hundred times each, before bed, and a mild sleeping pill if she was still anxious. She slept in the basement clubhouse most of the time with Bob on the bottom bunk, if his mother did not need him. He snored, reassuring her things were alright. If bad guys came in, they would have to deal with him first, plus she slept with her boot knife and walkie-talkie under her pillow. Propping her head on the lumps comforted her.

The clubhouse had been improved with a large television screen, video games, and better heat. Red, white, and blue lava lamps bubbled and glowed as night lights.

Oceanna and Bob came along close behind Maria. Bob sported a scary police officer vampire costume with green face paint, nerdy glasses without lenses, a white, button-down shirt and thin black tie, greased back hair, a set of handcuffs in his belt his mother lent him, and long, glow-in-the-dark fangs, painted on his mouth and chin. He kept spitting out the plastic fangs because he couldn't snack on the candy.

Oceanna chose a comfortable costume, crafting a set of lavender bat wings she altered from full-sized butterfly wings Maria found in a dumpster, with a fuzzy purple sweater, lavender grease paint on her face, long yellow fangs in paint, and a tall gold tiara with blinking lights that looked like diamonds.

When the haunted trio had all arrived, Maria rang the doorbell. When the door opened, they sang trick or treat; candy dropped into their sacks, the lady turned off the porch light and said good night.

"Okay, guys, we're done. I'm exhausted. We've walked for miles," said Oceanna, pointing back to their street.

"Yeah, my feet hurt. How about you, officer?" said Maria to Bob, who seemed to be dragging his feet. He smiled a brown, chocolate-covered smile and nodded.

The moonless sky was dark and cold. When they got home, Maria's house was dark, so she packed her stuff into the clubhouse, figuring her father had had a drink and gone to bed already. Since she was not tired, she would play in the basement with Bob rather than wake Ralphie up, sorting the favorite candy from the not so favorite, dark chocolate for light milk chocolate and gum for sour candy, put on her pajamas, and play cards. They all went to bed peacefully until Bob smelled smoke and saw fire.

Dolly stood, straight-backed and still, on her porch, wrapped in Bob's large overcoat, smoking a long cigarette, silently watching the flames grow at the rear of Maria's home. She watched Officer Cake arrive, lights flashing, jamming on the brakes, flinging the door open, pulling on leather gloves, and rushing in to help.

Bob ran down the street to his house and stood at the gate below his mother, watching the fire grow, wringing his hands, and rocking back and forth anxiously, wiping his tears from his cheeks, smudging his painted-on fangs.

The house popped and crackled as the flames roared up the walls to the roof. Black smoke billowed from the windows, flames flashing to the cedar shingles. A fire engine screamed up the narrow street. The rescue crew jumped from the truck, grabbed their kits, and moved to the front door. A long hose was screwed to the hydrant, the valve cranked open, and water began to shoot out at high velocity. The flames hissed and sizzled as the water hit.

Oceanna was carried out, unconscious, folded over a shoulder, blacked with ashes, and a singed terry cloth robe. Her feet were blistered. Laid out for triage on a blanket, she received oxygen while they cut the cloth for her skin. Officer Cake told them others might be in the back bedroom. They told her they had kicked in the bedroom door and seen two adult bodies in the rear bedroom, charred and lifeless. She checked Oceanna, who was becoming conscious, and asked her where Maria was, but she could not speak; her throat was dry.

She ran across the street, up the stairs, through the front door, searched the living room and kitchen, and leaped down the basement stairs to the clubhouse. Maria lay quietly on the top bunk, covered in flannel blankets, fast asleep, with her walkie-talkie tucked under her chin. Cake took her in her arms and sobbed.

C H A P T E R   3 2 :

CHRISTMAS END

T he chill of Christmas Eve felt good. The lights on Bob and Dolly's plastic tree twinkled festively. Bob hummed out of tune to the carols on the radio, dressed in a red plaid shirt and a green light-up bow tie. Rocking back and forth in front of the gas hearth, he remembered Nurse Ambrosia stringing lights around the tree in the nurse's station, becoming bright and giggly with each secret swig of gin. Her grey blond hair came loose from the bun, straggling down around her crow's feet eyes, lipstick spotting her yellow smile as she became sillier and less self-conscious. She shined for him. Blowing him private kisses from across the hall, winking now and then. Remembering her brought warmth to his heart. She was his angel.

Dolly sorted papers from a locked drawer bearing Bob's full name, birth certificate, shot records, trial papers, documents from his incarceration and custody, and doctor's reports about his mental state and potential dangers. She reread the yellowed newspaper clippings of the fire that killed his father, sealing Bob's fate, the release of the patient from the asylum, and his discharge papers. She included a five-page, handwritten letter to Officer Cake, folded and sealed in a Christmas card envelope, with a silver card tied with a back ribbon with a short poem about forgiveness. After loading the documents into a silver and black gift box, she tied it with a blood-red ribbon, tears running down her cheeks. She did not wipe them away. Several tears fell onto the box, staining the red ribbon.

She brushed her long gray hair with candlelight that flickered, reflecting brightly off the black and silver wallpaper on her bedroom walls. The four tall posts of her heavy wooden bedframe glistened with polish. The black satin sheets sparkled, and the air smelled of her favorite holiday incense, sandalwood. Her nightgown was silvery, low cut, and transparent. Her breasts were playing just under the silk. She spread red lipstick on her lips, hoping to entice a final kiss. She thought her reflection looked as ethereal as a ghost.

"Perfect," she whispered to herself.

"Bobby. Darling! Please make Mother a nice martini. We have to talk before you go to your party," Dolly called down to Bob, who was already mixing her drink.

She plopped down on the couch, tucked her feet under her thighs, and lit a smoke, leaving the gift box near the front door for Bob to deliver to Cake at the Christmas Party at Oceanna's place. She looked over the bottles of pills on the side table, shaking them for contentment. Nerves were acting up; she took a few into her mouth just as Bob arrived with her martini and washed them down.

"Mom looks pretty. Pretty hair," said Bob smiling broadly in anticipation of good eats and music he would pump out with the foot pedals on the player piano at the party.

"Bobby. I have to tell you a secret tonight before you go. Sit with me," she patted the cushion next to her. He sat, and she took his hands into hers. He squeezed her cold fingers gently and held on.

"Bobby, I have to tell you the truth about Daddy. You know I loved him. You remember I tried to make him happy, but he got so mean to us. He hit you, Bobby. It made you cry. Said mean things to you, do you remember, honey?" her tears dripped from her chin.

Bob nodded and frowned.

"Dad hurt me, Mom."

"I know he did, darling. And I couldn't stop him. Then one day, our magician, Grandma Blanch, helped me. She was smart and much stronger than I was then. You played with Oceanna that summer, remember? On the swings in the backyard?"

Bob let go of her hands and rubbed his palms together; his face lacked his usual smile. The corners of his mouth turned down.

"Bob, I had to do something to end the fight. It was us or him; I mean it. He was blind drunk. He could have shot us and forgotten it the next day—a monster in one of his rages. I told Blanch about the fights. She saw and cared for the bruises with her strange herbs and spells. Well darling, she offered to help one day to finish the problem and . . . we made a plan. I gave Daddy special medicine to make him sleep. I snuck it into his bottle of scotch. At first, it didn't seem to be working, and he was hitting me, but then he stopped and fell onto the floor. You were outside swinging and rocking as usual. Not hurting a fly, so I set the fire and picked you up, and we hid in the basement at Blanche's; your little clubhouse was our hideout until the firemen came, and thankfully, it was too late to save your father."

Dolly looked into Bob's frown. He licked his lips and fluttered his eyelids, and started to cry.

"Please forgive me, son. I had to Bobby; Dad lost his decency and took other women. I hated how you hid in the bedroom closet and saw what he did. You know."

Finishing her drink, she set the glass on the table and lit another smoke.

"My real regret is that they blamed you. That was not part of the plan! The neighbors said they saw you in the backyard before the fire started; you had played with matches once and lit the weeds on fire! I let them take you thinking after I got things straightened out, the pension and the house patched up; I could come to get you. They would not let me have you back, son. The doctors registered you as dangerous! The plan went to hell, and my life went with it. Blanch and I suffered for years together, then she died and left the house to Oceanna, and I thought of a new plan."

She stood, walked into the kitchen, grabbed two bottles of vodka, poured herself another glass, and placed one bottle on the coffee table. In one bottle, a ribbon of lavender swirled in spirals throughout, like it was alive.

She pulled a long black ribbon from around her neck and tied it carefully around the bottle as Bob watched her pale fingers.

"This is for Oceanna and Cake, darling. Very special, magical present for them. You deliver this with my best Christmas wishes. Okay?" she smiled faintly.

"I do it, Mom. Christmas for Anna."

"And I have to tell you more—one more secret for you to keep. I had to set a fire at Maria's house too. That was my new plan, to have you live with Oceanna. She is almost your sister because I loved Blanche Pontic, more than a friend. She loved you like a son, didn't she? I watched the ladies and looked in their windows to see if they were loving and good, treating each other nicely. Not like Dad, so they could take care of you when I was gone, and you could have Maria as your sister. Ralfie didn't take good care of Maria, right? I can see the beauty and a good heart in Officer Cake. So, tonight I give Emerald Cake to Oceanna and you to them. Now, you can have a sister and two mothers, see? When Vivian returned on Halloween, I was watching through the window; she got right into bed with him . . . I couldn't let her mess it up; I had to get rid of them both."

"What? What you say, Mom?" Bob asked, confused and frustrated that she wanted to tell ugly stories rather than go to the party.

"It's all in the box, Bobby, darling. I told the story in a letter to Cake. She will know what to do, and then some," she handed the spiced bottle of lavender vodka to Bob, walked him to the door, put a red kiss on his cheek, and handed him the box.

"I can't live like this anymore, honey. I'm a killer. They could come for me any day. Forgive Mother if you can. I love you. Give this all to Cake now. Don't forget. Merry Christmas, baby. Have fun," said Dolly as she aimed him down the porch steps, waved goodbye, watched him hustle down the street, and shut the door.

She removed a long vile of black honey from her pocket and poured herself another martini. She turned off the lights but left the tree lights blinking farewell.

Carrying the liquor into her shimmering bedroom, she looked herself over in the mirror again and felt exhausted and ready. She lifted the glass vile of inky potion to her lips, upended the vile, and drank the bitter medicine with a sigh. She opened the window and watched Bob disappear up the stairs into Oceanna's house, then climbed into her bed, arranged the sheets smoothly, and gave up.

CHAPTER 33:

LAVENDER DREAMS ON A STARRY NIGHT

Maria lay on her bunk in the basement watching movies while Oceanna cooked the holiday meal. Determined to make the holiday happy as much as possible, she cooked too much while trying to forget the losses. The burnt-out house that remained a grim reminder of their tragedy was finally cleared away by a large yellow tractor with a claw. Maria and Oceanna had watched from the porch swing, crying as the ribs crumbled into fragments, then were scooped up and hauled away, leaving an empty lot ready for a fresh future.

Maria begged the court to let her stay with Oceanna, and with Cakes' help, the wish was granted. Now she was the owner of an empty lot and a new family. Their heads had been too foggy, too grief-deprived to think clearly.

The sweet smells of a turkey roasting had brightened Maria's mood slightly, momentarily replacing the images of her father's funeral with thoughts of tasting good food and some level of emotional stability. Her appetite had been poor, and Oceanna hoped to change it tonight.

Keeping busy with holiday activities had allowed Oceanna to find relief from losing Viv. Vivian's family had taken the body back to California and refused to allow anyone to attend but family. Oceanna was secretly grateful; crying at funerals was not her wish. She could show her respect at home.

She cooked and cleaned and set a beautiful table with as much bounty as possible. Maria had picked out the biggest tree she could find. They had hauled it home from the Christmas tree lot on the corner with Bob's help and trimmed it with decorations Maria's class roommates had made for her. The Cake had hung gold stars and doggie-shaped ornaments and placed the treetop with a large angel lit with a bulb that blinked the colors of the rainbow.

From the corner of her eye, Maria saw a flash of paw, orange fir peeking under the outside door and heard a soft peep like a small kitten mewing. Then a fat paw slid under the door and clawed to get in. She jumped carefully off the top bunk and tip-toed to the door. She breathed and stuck her finger out to test the paw's pink pads. She stroked the long clear claws, smiling for the first time in a week. The animal peeped again. She cooed, praying she would not scare it away. She enticed skillfully with a string.

Slowly, the cat leaned against the door, and a large whiskered face with clear green eyes stared up at her. Her heart leaped. It paraded in as confidently as though it had lived there the whole time. Rubbing her cheek on the door frame, the long white whiskers spread out from her face like a fan. She reared up on her hind legs to play, and her tall ears reached above the doorknob.

"I'm gonna name you Magic, kitty. I already have a horse named Dream and a dog named Zsa-Zsa. I've been looking for you. You must have been watching me all the time," she burst into tears.

Maria sat cross-legged and held her hand out to pet her. The cat climbed into her lap and rolled onto her back to play, showing her belly full of new kittens, almost ready to come. Maria petted the round head, stroked the thick fir down her back and tail, and then tried to pick her up to show Oceanna. She had to drape the cat over her shoulders to gather her fully. Magic's legs stretched down to her waist. She purred so loud it tickled Maria's ears, making her laugh. She tramped up the stairs, walked into the kitchen, and sang.

"Look what I found!" Grinning ear to ear and crying. The enormous creature relaxed and easily draped about her neck.

"Wow! You finally found it!" Oceanna stood gob-smacked with the large spoon in her hand.

"She just showed up! And I think she is going to have kittens! I wished for her many times, and now she just came in. She loves me already."

"Wow. She is magnificent. You are really getting a wonderful gift this Christmas. She is probably hungry and smells the turkey. We have enough to go around for sure. Better feed her so she'll stay. Have you named her?"

"I'm calling her Magic because she is my magic wish."

It took time for Oceanna to lift the purring beast off Maria's shoulders and set her on the feet. The cat's tail unfolded, bobbing as high as the kitchen counter.

"I'll get the gibbets cut up for her. She is a giant, and if she is having babies, she will need a lot of feeding and care from you, Maria," she said, wiping her face with a dish towel, brushing back her bangs, and hugging her.

"Good to cry, good to cry for a while," she said, also bringing herself to tears. The cat circled them both, pressing her long body into them in a feline embrace.

Four heavy knocks rattled at the front door, indicating that Bob had arrived. Maria ran to the door, leading Bob into the kitchen to see her new friend.

"Oh, big kitty!" he laughed, clapped his hands together, and reluctantly put out his fingers to pet her. She walked up and rubbed herself on his knee, leaning her full weight into him. He handed Oceanna the bottle his mother sent and showed her the box.

"Merry Christmas, Mom said," smiling wide, he gazed at the table full of food and licked his lips. She took the bottle from him with thanks and directed him to put the box from his mother under the tree with the other gifts. He trotted into the living room, tossed the box among the others, and stepped to the piano for his fun. He opened the piano, chose a Christmas song, carefully lodged the player pegs into the slots, and began to pump the pedals. The roll began to spin with a wheeze. He rocked right and left, sitting on the stool, humming out of tune gayly.

Another knock on the door announced Cake and Zsa-Zsa. They pushed open the door and stepped in without waiting for Maria to answer it. The Cake held up a wreath with blinking lights that looked like cranberries and a glass plate with a large, homemade sweet potato pie, still warm.

Maria was sitting on the bean bag chairs with Magic surrounding her in a sea of pale fire. Zsa-Zsa stopped momentarily in shock, then walked slowly to her cat's nose, sniffed her lightly in a playful greeting, and sat with them. Maria hugged the dog's neck and buried her face in her thick black coat. Magic purred and licked her paws.

"Well, now. It looks like we have a new member of our little gang," said Cake as she entered the kitchen.

"Maria is calling her Magic because it was her wish for Christmas, and the cat is going to have kittens. Extra!" smiled Oceanna. She held up the lavender Vodka from Dolly. Holding it to the light gave Cake the full view of lavender spiraling through it.

"Well?" She offered it with a grin. "Are you ready for whatever this is, Em?"

"I love adventure, as you know. I don't think it will kill us. Do you?" she gave a broad smile.

"I think a toast is in order, at any rate. That child is feeling something positive again. And having you around has helped me feel better. I wanted to tell you that." Oceanna blushed. She grabbed a couple of wide martini glasses from the shelf and poured the strange brew into them. It fizzed and glowed. Cake set the hot pie on the table, catching the dog's attention.

"Here is to one adventure after another, Officer Cake," said Oceanna, holding up her glass for a clink.

"And here is to you for making it all work beautifully," said Cake.

They looked at each other. Eyed the cocktail, braced themselves, interlocked their arms, and drank. The burn of the lavender entered their heads on contact. Heat spread from their throats, and chills ran down their spines. They opened their eyes and looked at each other, not an inch apart, frozen in place. Cake leaned down and put her lips gently onto Oceanna's.

Thrilled and surprised, the kiss grew deeper. Cake took her in her arms, pulled her in tightly, and fell in love. Oceanna was overwhelmed, felt disoriented, and saw fireworks. When they opened their eyes, lavender halos surrounded them. They laughed, danced close to Bob's piano tunes, and kissed again.

The bats squeezed tight to each other for warmth and fluttered in the tower's eves, tasting the chill of winter with fluttering red tongues, and looked at the stars with bright yellow eyes. Maria rolled herself up in fir and soft purrs while Zsa-Zsa drooled, hoping for a piece of the sweet potato pie.

And Dream, The Blue Ribbon Mare, floated among peach-colored clouds, reared up and boxed at the stars with her hooves, then galloped off into the night to run a victory lap around the moon.

The End.